WISHING
FOR THE
RANCHER'S LOVE

Bride Ships Series
A Reluctant Bride
The Runaway Bride
A Bride of Convenience
Almost a Bride

Orphan Train Series
An Awakened Heart: A Novella
With You Always
Together Forever
Searching for You

Beacons of Hope Series
Out of the Storm: A Novella
Love Unexpected
Hearts Made Whole
Undaunted Hope
Forever Safe
Never Forget

Hearts of Faith Collection
The Preacher's Bride
The Doctor's Lady
Rebellious Heart

Michigan Brides Collection
Unending Devotion
A Noble Groom
Captured by Love

Historical
Luther and Katharina
Newton & Polly

HIGH COUNTRY RANCH SERIES

Wishing for the Rancher's Love

Jody Hedlund

NORTHERN LIGHTS PRESS

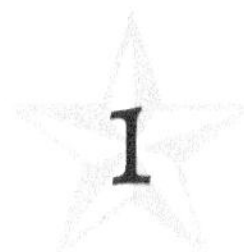

1

"I'm going as fast as I can." Clementine Oakley purposefully stirred the boiling caramel mixture slower. It was almost done and ready to pour, but she wasn't about to tell Grady Worth that.

Grady leaned against the hallway entrance of the small work area at the back of the general store, tapping one of his boots impatiently. His arms were folded across his chest, pulling his flannel shirt tight and outlining his broad chest and thickly muscled biceps.

Not that she cared about his broad chest and thickly muscled biceps. Or how mussed his dark-brown hair was without his Stetson. Or how the layer of scruff on his face made him look rugged. Or how the dark brown of his eyes was always so mysterious and appealing.

She didn't care one ounce about Grady. He'd been

her nemesis for years, and with every passing day over the two weeks since she'd started renting the room above the store, he'd grown more antagonistic.

"You're taking twice as long as usual." His voice was loaded with irritation.

"Am not."

"I can tell you slowed down."

She was tempted to go even slower, but she didn't want to ruin the batch of caramel, which needed constant stirring while it was boiling. Instead, she shifted so he had full view of her pretty face and womanly figure. "Admit it. You like when I go slow. Then you get to admire me for longer."

He snorted. "You have plenty of other men giving you attention and don't need mine."

He wasn't wrong on that score. She knew well enough that men found her blond-red hair, green eyes, and willowy body attractive. In the high country of Colorado in 1879, where men still outnumbered women, the attention wasn't anything new.

She tucked a loose strand of her long hair back into the messy bun she wore, which was even looser and messier after a long day working in the store. "You sound jealous."

"You wish."

It was her turn to snort. She'd lost count of how many times they'd had this sort of petty conversation.

Sometimes she wished they could turn back the years and return to being friends, like they'd been after he'd moved to Breckenridge eight years ago. At the time, he'd been fourteen and she'd been twelve, and those had been the carefree years before his mom had died.

Of course, things had started changing even before Mrs. Worth had died, but after she'd passed away three years ago, Grady and Clementine had gone from friends to enemies. Now they had nothing left between them but dissension.

Clementine swirled the mixture of molasses, sugar, chocolate, milk, and butter in the large saucepan on the old corner stove. The combination was gooey and rich and chewy, and the caramels were a favorite among her customers.

They'd been one of Mrs. Worth's earliest confectionery creations and one of the first the dear woman had taught her.

Grady shoved away from the hallway entrance and straightened to all six feet, three inches of brawny solidness gained from his hard work operating the town's livery. As he took a step into the room, he filled it with his overpowering presence.

It didn't help that the lean-to was small and crowded. With its original log walls and slanted ceiling, it was crammed full of crates of goods waiting to be unloaded in the store. She hardly had space to turn around without bumping into something.

With only one small window on the back wall, the area was gloomy, and she almost always needed a lantern to work. And it almost always smelled like coffee beans and musty potatoes and onions, especially when she wasn't making her candy.

It was hard to believe the room had served as a living area for the Worths when they'd first opened the store. The other little room off to one side that was now a telegram and post office had once been a bedroom for Mr. and Mrs. Worth. Grady had used the dormer upstairs as a bedroom, and eventually it had become a storage room.

Mr. Worth had cleared out the dormer and offered it to Clementine to rent after her ma had died in May. With the need to care for her ma no longer tying her to High Country Ranch—High C Ranch, as it was known—she could have moved to town so she didn't have to ride back and forth to work at the store.

However, she'd stayed at the ranch—hadn't been able to force herself to leave, even after Maverick had married his best friend's sister, Hazel.

At first Clementine had wanted to be there to help take care of the place and be close to her twin sister Clarabelle. However, Clarabelle had met and fallen in love with Franz Meyer back in June and moved away to be with him.

Then their adopted brother Ryder had needed assistance taking care of baby Boone over the rest of the summer until his mail-order bride had arrived. So Clementine had remained at home to be close enough to ride to Ryder's ranch several days a week to help with the baby.

After that, Clementine had considered Mr. Worth's offer again, but her other adopted brother, Tanner, had needed help doctoring the woman he loved back from an injury. Once Maisy had healed, the two had left for the East and would likely be gone all winter.

Maverick and Hazel claimed they loved having her live with them. But with Hazel being pregnant and due next spring, they would soon have their own little family to occupy them, and Clementine feared she would be even more of an outsider.

That lonely day at the end of October, Clementine had been at High C Ranch making a batch of candy, and with the emptiness of the house taunting her, she'd broken down in tears.

The realization had hit her hard that she was the only one of her siblings who wasn't married. She'd never imagined she'd be the last of her brothers and sisters to find love. She supposed they hadn't imagined it either, since she was the most outgoing and social of her siblings.

As she'd stood there in the kitchen, she'd asked herself what was wrong with her that she didn't have someone to love the way her siblings did. The feeling that she'd struggled with for so long—that she wasn't likeable enough—had resurfaced, making her need to get away and do something different with her life.

She'd gone to town the next day and accepted Mr. Worth's offer to rent the room. She'd moved in a day later and settled in over the last couple of weeks, cleaning the place and making it a cozy home.

The trouble was that she no longer had the big ranch kitchen to use for making the candy she sold in Worth's General Store. Now she had a less-than-ideal situation where she created her candy in the crowded back room. She was grateful Mr. Worth had offered to let her use the old stove. He'd even told her she could come over to the house and make her candy there.

But so far, she'd managed well enough. After all, if Mrs. Worth had been able to make her goodies in the lean-to room after first moving to Breckenridge, Clementine could do it too.

If only she didn't have to worry about Grady rushing her.

Grady stepped farther into the room. "I don't have all night to stand here and wait for you."

On a Thursday night in mid-November, with the temperature having dropped below freezing, she knew exactly where Grady wanted to be.

"I didn't ask you to wait." She reached for the greased

pan resting on the worktable next to the stove. "I don't need a nursemaid watching over me."

"That's debatable." His tone took on a cocky ring, and he started to twirl a key attached to a small leather strip around his finger.

"Go, Grady."

"You know I would if I could."

"I'm not stopping you."

"My dad will give me a whupping if I leave you here by yourself."

"Whupping? You're not five, even if you sometimes act like you are."

He released another snort.

She couldn't hold back the beginning of a grin. Although she missed their friendship, she could admit there were times when she took great enjoyment from the zingers they threw at each other.

He stopped beside the stove and peeked into the pot at the caramel. "Dad gave me the duty of making sure the store is locked up every night, and I intend to do it."

No doubt Grady was checking how far she had to go before the caramel was ready to pour out to cool. He'd watched his mom make candy often enough that he wasn't entirely ignorant of the process.

"I know you can go faster, Clementine"—the irritation was back in his voice—"so stop delaying."

She released an exasperated exhale. "Give me the key,

and I'll lock up after myself."

He flipped the key in a circle again and pressed his lips together. He had a tiny scar underneath his bottom lip from an ice-skating accident long ago. She'd always liked the scar—thought it gave his face texture, made his mouth more manly.

She held out her hand for the key.

He paused in twirling it but didn't immediately give it to her.

She lunged for the key as best she could while still stirring the caramel.

He easily lifted the key out of her reach.

She hopped and gripped the strip.

But in the next instant, he switched it into his other hand, even farther from her reach. All the while, his lips curved into a half smirk.

She didn't care about his mouth anymore. Not that she ever had. But especially not now. The only thing she wanted to do to his mouth was wipe the smirk off. "Just give me the key."

He dangled it in the air above her. "Promise you'll take it over to Dad just as soon as you finish here?"

"Yes, of course."

"The front door is already locked, so you only need to lock the back."

"Yes, Grady. I realize that."

He hesitated a beat longer, then tossed the key onto

the worktable with a clatter. Before she could stop him, he reached down into the bowl with the fruit-nut mixture that would go into the caramel, swiped up a finger of the concoction, then popped it into his mouth.

"Hey! That's disgusting." She swatted at him.

But he was already dodging away from her with the same finesse and ease he showed on the ice. He rounded a stack of crates, hopped over another, and was at the back door before she could try to swat him again.

"How many times do I have to tell you to wash your hands first?"

With his finger stuck in his mouth, he mumbled something—certainly not an apology. No, Grady Worth never apologized for anything. He was too stubborn and proud and smart for his own good.

She was tempted to toss her wooden spoon full of caramel at his retreating back, but she didn't relish having more to clean up than was already there. So she only glared at him as he opened the back door and stepped through, tossing another smirk her way as he did so.

As soon as the door closed and he was gone, she shook her head, then concentrated on the last steps of making the caramel. Within minutes, she had mixed in the fruit and nuts, poured the thick layer into the waiting pan, and spread it out. She let it cool while she washed the sauce pot and utensils. As she picked up a knife to cut the caramel into squares, the bell from the door at the front of the store tinkled.

She halted. Grady had said he'd already locked the front door. Had he forgotten?

Grady might be irritating and frustrating, but he was too responsible to neglect something so important.

She peered into the short hallway that led away from the lean-to. A faded calico curtain hung across the access to the storefront, acting as a divider and providing some privacy from the store's customers.

Had someone come inside to shop, even though the sign on the door read *closed* and even though the place was obviously dark and deserted for the evening?

She listened carefully, but the only sound she could hear was the sudden thumping of her heart.

Maybe the tinkling bell was nothing. Maybe a gust of wind had rattled the door. Or maybe someone passing by outside had triggered the bell. Whatever had happened, she couldn't worry about it.

She lowered the knife into the fudge and began to cut.

At a thud and the sound of something falling to the floor in the storefront, she froze, her eyes darting again to the hallway and the calico curtain separating her from whoever was in there.

Because someone had come into the store. There was no doubt about that now.

She swallowed and pushed down a lump that was

threatening to lodge in her throat. Then before she allowed her imagination to run wild, she swiped up the lantern from the table and started forward, knife in hand. It wasn't a big or a sharp knife, but it made her feel a little better to have it.

When she reached the end of the hallway, she stared at the curtain, wishing she could see through it. "Hello? Is someone there?"

Footsteps plodded quickly, the bell tinkled again, and then the door closed sharply.

Clementine was already pushing aside the curtain and racing into the front room. Light from the lantern revealed a deserted store, but she crossed directly to the door, swung it open, and stepped outside into the chilly darkness.

Breckenridge's main thoroughfare was busy for the evening hour, with men returning from the nearby mines to the hotels, boarding houses, and saloons.

She held the lantern high, hoping to see someone rushing away or looking guilty. But everyone seemed to be in a hurry, and no one looked particularly guilty of trying to break into Worth's General Store.

After several more seconds of scanning the people in the area, she returned to the familiar interior of the store. As she closed the door, she surveyed the floor-to-ceiling shelves that lined the walls, then the double-sided set of shelves at the center of the room.

All it took was a single glance, since she was so familiar with where everything in the store was located. The bolts of fabric, thread, buttons, and other sewing notions were organized neatly to the right of the door. The ready-made clothing and hats came next. After that, the shelves were stocked with linens, blankets, towels, and canvas that the miners needed. Ropes, ammunition, kerosene, whips, harnesses, and more filled the shelves on the back wall to overflowing. Most of the foodstuff in cans, tins, and bottles lined the shelves to the left of the door.

Several glass display units were strategically placed in front of the wall shelves, and one near the front of the store contained her candy. Jars of various sizes and shapes on the top were filled with hard candy sticks, rock candy, comfits, drops, and pulled creams. The more elaborate chocolates, caramels, candied fruit, almond hardbake, and other creations were displayed inside the unit on platters, arranged beautifully to entice customers into buying the candy.

Nothing appeared to be out of order . . . except for something near the candy jars.

She veered toward the display and lifted the lantern higher to find a single silk red rose lying on the glass countertop.

"What on earth?" She set down the lantern and her knife and then picked up the silk flower that looked as though it had come off a fancy bonnet. A ribbon with a small slip of paper dangled from the short stem.

How odd.

She turned over the paper to find simplistic, messy handwriting. "I hope you like the gifts."

Gifts?

Her thoughts flew back to the past week and the items she'd found—a pretty ribbon tied to one of her spatulas, a bowl of fresh eggs on the worktable, and a page of poetry that appeared to have been ripped from a book.

Were those the gifts?

She hadn't known what to think about the items she'd found, and at first had assumed Mr. Worth had given them to her. But when she'd thanked him for the eggs, he'd denied knowing anything about them.

She'd thought about confronting Grady. But he would never be an admirer—secret or otherwise. And he would never leave the items to be nice to her. To tease her, yes. But never to be thoughtful.

She twisted the silk rose around in her hand. If Mr. Worth and Grady hadn't left her the gifts, then who? Who would have gone to the trouble? And why?

At the strange feeling of being watched, the skin at the back of her neck prickled. Her gaze darted to the front windows. She expected someone to be standing there, peering inside. But only a horse and rider passed by on the street, and the fellow wasn't looking in her direction.

Was Milton Fogg leaving the gifts? The miner turned newspaper owner had been trying to win her over for the past few months. The man simply didn't appeal to her. And it wasn't just because of his large eyes and nose. He was at least ten years older than her, seemed set in his ways, and was too serious. But he was persistent and had asked her again just yesterday to go to dinner with him.

What about Jeremy Usher? The blacksmith's assistant was decently good-looking with his sandy-blond hair and blue eyes. But at times, he struck her as childish, as though he hadn't quite grown up yet even though he was twenty. He made a point of visiting her at the store every day, buying a piece of her candy each time he came in.

Had either of those two men been responsible for leaving her the gifts over the past week or so? Yes, the gifts had started about a week ago.

She studied the handwriting. Knowing how prolific Milton was with his writing, she couldn't imagine him having such messy handwriting. But Jeremy was less educated and might not know how to read or write well. It was possible he was trying to do something nice for her, although he didn't seem the type of man who would think about anyone besides himself.

The real question was, how had the fellow gotten inside the store if Grady had locked the door? And if the person had known she was in the lean-to making candy, why hadn't he come and talked to her and given her the flower? Why keep it a secret?

She glanced around the store again as if she could discover the answers to all her questions, but nothing made sense.

If he'd hoped to make her feel special with the silk rose, it hadn't worked. Instead, it had unsettled her more than anything.

With rapid steps, she returned to the door, locked the bolt, then hastened back into the lean-to, where she finished cutting the caramel and covered it with a towel.

When she was done with the last of her tidying and wiping, she grabbed her coat from the hook next to the door. As she stuffed her arms into it, something in the pocket poked her. She slipped her hand inside, and her fingers connected with the silky petals of another rose.

She pulled it out to find that it was nearly identical to the red rose she'd found on the candy display case, also with a ribbon holding a slip of paper. Had the person come inside the back door while she'd been at the front of the store?

A chill crept up her spine.

She turned the note around to find more of the same messy handwriting. This time the message read: "I'd like you to be mine."

As if the rose were scorching her fingers, she tossed it. It fell to the floor, and she could only stare at it as another chill rippled through her.

Normally, she didn't mind a little bit of extra attention. But whoever was doing this was going too far.

"I don't like that you left Clementine in the store alone," Dad said from his spot at the long, elegant table across from Grady.

Grady had been waiting for the admonition during the entire meal, knowing his dad wouldn't let him get away with leaving Clementine to lock up on her own. He finished swallowing a last bite before responding. "Clementine insisted on having the key."

"It doesn't matter. I don't want you to leave her alone there." Dad had discarded his suit coat and bow tie but still wore his navy vest with his shirt sleeves rolled up to his elbows. His dark brown hair was cut short and fashionably styled, and his beard was also neatly groomed. Without any wrinkles or any gray hair, Dad always looked younger than his age, as though he were thirty instead of forty-five.

Grady pushed around a last bite of stew with his

spoon, the clinking loud in the dining room, which was too formal, too quiet, and too elegant for bachelors like them.

The room was still fancy the way Mom had decorated it, with cheerful yellow wallpaper and white lace everywhere—the tablecloth, the curtains, the doilies on the sideboard, and the rug beneath the table. Even the dishes they ate off were white with a scalloped edge that resembled lace.

In contrast, their meal had been anything but fancy. It never was anymore. Tonight had been canned stew. In fact, most nights their fare consisted of something from a can that only required warming up on the stove.

It was a far cry from the elaborate home-baked meals Mom used to make. The thought didn't bring the sharp grief that it used to. Now it only brought a sense of nostalgia. And a sense of sadness for his dad.

"I'm sorry." Grady placed his spoon on the pretty plate.

Dad took a sip of his coffee and then paused with the cup suspended above the matching white saucer. His eyes, although kind, held disapproval. "Clementine lives with us now, son, and we need to look after her."

Grady pushed down his irritation and answered calmly. "She's not living with us. She's renting the room—"

"Close enough." Dad gingerly set the cup down, the

liquid likely lukewarm now, if not entirely cold.

Grady wasn't sure why Dad persisted in drinking from the white scalloped cups that never kept the coffee hot more than a minute. The cup was also so small that a man could only take two sips before draining it dry.

Of course, Mom had always used the fine china for after-dinner coffee to go along with one of her delicious pastries. But it had been three years since they'd had the pleasure of eating anything she'd made. Even so, dad continued to use the delicate cups for after-dinner coffee.

Grady studied his dad's large hands circling the porcelain. It was past time for his dad to let go of all the customs and habits he'd kept with Mom. He needed to move on. That was becoming more obvious with every passing day.

Grady cleared his throat, wanting to say as much, but as usual, the words stuck in his chest.

"Clementine is more than just a boarder, Grady." Dad rubbed his thumb around the rim of the cup. "She's like family."

"I understand." Or at least, Grady *tried* to understand. But he never really had understood why Clementine had become part of his family, especially since she'd had such a large and loving family of her own—her pa, ma, four brothers, and her twin sister— when he'd only had his dad and mom and no siblings.

Yes, her pa had passed away early in the year, and her

ma had followed not long after him. But Clementine had grown up with more family than most and had always been close to them. She didn't need his family too.

But just like his thoughts about their outdated supper habits, he kept his opinions about Clementine to himself—or at least, mostly so.

"I just wish she'd come over and join us for a meal." Dad lifted his cup and took another sip.

Grady's muscles were starting to tense with the longing to make his way over to Mill Pond, where the fellows would be waiting for him to start a game of hockey. But having gone out the past couple of evenings, he didn't want to leave Dad alone for the third night in a row. The dark winter nights were long and lonely, and his dad liked his company, maybe even relied on it.

Not that Grady didn't enjoy sitting in front of the warm stove and playing backgammon or checkers or cards. He appreciated their easy camaraderie, the stories Dad told, the laughter they shared, and the deep discussions they sometimes had.

But when the ice froze over, Grady loved being out on it. He always had.

"I've invited Clementine almost every night." Dad sighed as he placed his cup down with a gentle clink. "And she always tells me she doesn't want to be a bother."

Grady almost snorted. Clementine didn't care if she bothered him. In fact, she seemed to make it her life's mission to bother him.

"Maybe if *you* told her you'd like her to come for supper . . ." Dad said tentatively.

Grady shook his head. He loved his dad and would do just about anything for him. But he had to draw the line somewhere, and that somewhere was with Clementine. "She's busy most evenings making candy."

"That's what I'm afraid of. She'll get too wrapped up in her work and won't leave time for fun."

"Don't worry about that." Grady couldn't keep the edge from his tone. "She leaves time for fun when she wants to." She'd walked over to Mill Pond the past two nights. The first evening, she'd watched the hockey game, but last night she'd spent the entire time flirting with several fellows.

He'd tried to ignore her and focus on the game, but wherever Clementine Oakley went, she was hard to miss. Not only was she always the most beautiful woman in the crowd, but she was the most outgoing and vivacious, laughing and talking and joking with everyone. And the guys all loved her and were drawn to her like children eager to get their grubby hands on a piece of sweet candy.

He wished she'd stay away from the games, from the skating, and from the fellows. But Clementine thrived on attention.

"Maybe you can go over and see if she'd like to join us for cards?" Dad's brow lifted above his brown eyes—

eyes so much like Grady's.

Pressure swelled inside Grady. He wanted to be a good son—the best son he could be. He'd tried to step in and take Mom's place, tried to keep Dad occupied and busy. But there were days—and nights—when he felt as though he was failing to be all that his dad needed, like the past couple of nights. And again tonight.

"I was planning to get in a game of hockey." Grady tossed out the words as nonchalantly as possible.

"Oh."

Did that one word hint at disappointment, or was Grady imagining it? "But I can skip—"

"No, no. You go on." His dad waved a hand. "We'll finish that game of checkers when you get back."

Grady hesitated. "You're sure?"

"Of course I'm sure." His dad's voice contained forced cheer.

Grady didn't move from his chair. He needed to cancel his plans for the evening and spend the time with Dad. That's what he needed to do.

He rolled one of his shoulders, stiff from the bruise he'd gotten the previous night. "On second thought, I think I'll skip the hockey. I'm sore—"

"No." The one word was sharp—sharper than usual. Dad picked up the white cup and drained it. As he set it down, he shifted it gently one way and then the other. Then he reached up and began to undo the top button of his shirt, stretching his neck as he did so.

Uh-oh. Whenever Dad loosened his shirt, that meant he had something important to say—usually something unpleasant, something Grady wouldn't like.

"Grady, I've been thinking . . ." And those were the words Dad always used when he started with that something important and unpleasant.

Grady swallowed the trepidation.

"I'm thinking," his dad said again, tugging at his shirt collar as though it was attempting to strangle him, "that I'd like to propose a challenge, a contest of sorts between us."

Grady sat up straighter. "Challenge? Contest?"

"I'm not getting any younger and neither are you." His dad made the announcement as if the news should come as a surprise to Grady.

But Grady had felt older this year as he'd joined the fellows for hockey, especially because he was one of the oldest of the group now. Most of the others his age had moved on or gotten married.

Dad met his gaze head-on. "My challenge is that you find true love by Christmas. And if you do, I'll loan you the money for the building next door so you can start the hardware store you've been talking about."

Grady's pulse slowed as he tried to make sense of his dad's words. His dad was a savvy entrepreneur and had investments all throughout Breckenridge, more property and businesses than most people knew about—several house rentals, a boarding house, other business buildings he rented along Main Street and some of the side streets. He also had substantial amounts of property and businesses over in Georgetown, where they'd first lived when moving to Colorado.

After watching his dad buy up land and expand his investments, Grady wanted to do the same. So when the pharmacist who owned the drug store next to the general store had started constructing a new place on Ridge Street, Grady had offered to buy the old building. With a surge of new miners coming into the area, Grady figured the town could use a hardware store that sold items builders and miners alike needed.

After having to purchase two new carriages over the past year, Grady had fallen short of what the pharmacist was asking for the old building. But being a friendly fellow, he'd given Grady until Christmas to come up with the funds. After that, he planned to find another buyer. And Grady knew who that buyer would be. Dad.

Grady shook his head, the determination to make his own way rising up within him. "You know I don't want charity—"

"It's not charity." His dad's voice turned hard. "It's a loan. You'll have to pay me back with interest."

His dad knew he'd already tried to get the bank to give him a loan, but they hadn't been willing since he hadn't proven himself yet with the livery.

"So you'll give me the loan"—Grady couldn't keep his own voice from turning hard—"but only with a bribe attached to it."

"Not a bribe. A challenge."

Grady shrugged. "It sounds like a bribe."

"Look at it as an incentive." His dad's eyes had narrowed in that shrewd way he had about him—a shrewdness that had helped him become a very wealthy man.

"I don't need any incentives."

"Then you'll lose out on the building."

Grady crossed his arms and held his dad's gaze. "I'm not rushing love just so I can get a loan from you."

"I don't want you to rush. All I want you to do is make an effort."

Maybe the challenge wasn't so crazy after all. Maybe it was even reasonable. Christmas was still at least six weeks away. That was plenty of time to make an effort to get to know a young woman in the area and start a serious courtship. Even though there weren't hordes of eligible women to choose from, surely he could find one he was attracted to.

But doing so would mean leaving Dad behind more evenings. Marriage would make the situation worse. Then who would Dad have? He'd be alone, sipping cold coffee from his white china cup by himself every supper.

Grady shook his head, but before he could protest, his dad tugged on his collar again, and this time his neck was turning red. "Guess what I'm trying to say is that maybe I need to make an effort too."

Grady opened his mouth to respond but then quickly closed it. What was his dad saying? That he needed to find a woman?

"Your mom . . ." he started, then stopped and cleared his throat. "Before she died, she made me promise I'd get remarried."

"Sounds like something Mom would want." Even if she had struggled with melancholy, she'd always had a beautiful and kind soul. Of course she'd have wanted her husband to find happiness again.

"She didn't want me to be alone."

Grady had never considered the possibility of his dad getting remarried, but it made sense. After all, his dad was still young and had needs. Not that Grady wanted to think about those needs, but still . . .

Dad's neck was still red, and now Grady knew why.

"I didn't want to promise your mom anything," Dad continued. "I thought I'd be just fine alone."

"But you're not?"

"Oh, I'm fine," he said hastily. "But what I'm realizing is that I'm holding you back. You're not going out and finding love and making a life for yourself because you're worried about being here for me."

"I want to be here for you."

"I know you do, son." His dad's brow furrowed above sad eyes. "But I can't let you make that sacrifice for me—"

"It's not a sacrifice."

"Grady, listen. I need to move on. And so the challenge is as much for me as for you."

Move on. Hadn't Grady been thinking that very thing just a short while ago? Not necessarily that his dad needed to move on to a new wife. But what if doing so would help him release Mom and all the memories? What if doing so would bring him happiness and companionship?

Maybe this *would* be good for both of them. In fact, Grady suspected his mom wouldn't have pushed his dad for the promise unless she'd been certain he would be happy with another woman in his life.

If Mom had believed it, then Grady had to believe it too. In fact, in seeing the loneliness in his dad tonight, he knew it was true. His dad needed to get married again.

Grady sat back in his chair and let his muscles relax. "So, what's your part of the challenge?"

His dad eased out a tight breath. "If you find love first, you get the loan to buy the building. If I find love first, then I get to play matchmaker for you."

Immediately, Grady sat forward and shook his head. "No way. You'll pick Clementine."

Dad's brows shot up. "How do you know?"

"Because I'm not an idiot. I know you're already playing matchmaker with me and her and have been for a while."

"I love Clementine, and I know you do too."

"No, I don't. We can't stand each other."

Dad didn't say anything, which meant he was sticking by what he'd said.

"That's not fair." Grady didn't care if his voice was slightly whiny.

"Go ahead and find someone else you care about even half as much as her." Dad's lips quirked into the beginning of a grin. "You know you won't."

"Sure I will."

"I'd like to see it."

"You will."

"Then we're agreed on the terms of the contest?" His dad stuck out a hand.

Grady hesitated. He wasn't planning to end up with Clementine. He'd rather marry a pecking hen than her. All the more incentive to win the contest. Not only would he get the building and be able to start up a hardware store, but he'd also get to choose his own bride.

He reached for his dad's hand and shook. "Guess that means I'll need to fall in love soon."

His dad squeezed hard, then released him, his grin breaking free. "Good luck."

Grady couldn't hold back a grin of his own. "Good luck to you too."

Clementine tried not to stare at the hockey players dodging around on the ice, but her gaze kept straying there anyway. They were all so strong and fast and good-looking. Even Grady had an appeal. Like the others, he'd shed his coat and rolled up his sleeves almost to his elbows. She'd never known forearms could be so manly, but his were most definitely eye-catching, with their flexing tendons, pulsing veins, and popping muscles.

Not only was he a strongly built man, but his presence both on and off the ice was commanding—particularly on the ice. He skated and played hockey as if he owned the place and everyone and everything belonged to him. It wasn't arrogance. But it was close.

Regardless, she could admit he was the best player on either team—probably the most experienced, the strongest, and the most decisive. He was fun to watch.

But she didn't want to give him the pleasure of

knowing she enjoyed seeing him play. He would never let her live it down, would forever be teasing her about ogling him.

Beside her, on the sideline of the pond, Willa was chattering with the fellows they'd mingled with over the past couple of evenings. Although Clementine was attempting to stay part of the conversation, she was distracted by the game . . . and Grady.

Willa laughed at something and then nudged Clementine. "Isn't that right, Clementine?"

Grady was in the process of ducking underneath the arm of one player while hitting the puck with his hockey stick, and she didn't want to take her attention off his fluid yet strong moves. But she forced herself to smile brightly at her friend. "Is what right?"

Willa twisted one of her long dark locks of hair and smiled coyly at the fellow beside her. "We'll be at the dance tomorrow night."

"Oh my, we wouldn't miss it." Clementine bestowed a smile on the two men.

"Then I claim the first dance with you." The taller of the two—John—reached for Clementine's mittened hand.

She allowed him to capture it. What harm was there in letting him hold her hand for a few seconds?

He seemed decent enough, had explained that he and his friends were new to the area and had come to mine and strike it rich. He had a nice-looking face, even if his mustache was sparse as if he was trying to grow facial hair but hadn't been able to sprout it yet.

So far, he and his friends had been lively and fun.

John swung her hand. "I don't want to wait until tomorrow to dance. How about if we dance right here tonight?"

"Here?" Clementine glanced around at the others crowded along the pond. "Tonight?"

Mill Pond was only two blocks away from the general store on Main Street—close enough that Clementine had been able to walk to the hockey games. The trip was much shorter and easier than riding into town from the ranch as she'd had to do in previous years. That was another advantage to living in town—she could join in more of the evening activities.

The pond was a leveled-out area of grassy embankment near the Blue River. Someone had created the pond a number of years ago for ice-skating, keeping the water level only a couple of inches deep so it would freeze over more quickly than the river.

In November, when the daily temperatures often rose above freezing, the pond sometimes melted during the day. It stayed more consistently frozen throughout the winter than the river. During particularly snowy times, tents were erected over the pond to keep it free of too much accumulation.

Over the years, it had become a popular place for the young people in the area to gather. Lined with lanterns hung from lampposts strategically placed around the perimeter, the pond was busy with clusters of onlookers cheering on the game and others who'd simply come to mingle.

And now, apparently, John wanted to have a dance there.

He lifted her hand into a waltz-like pose—at least, she thought it was waltz-like, since she'd never actually waltzed. Then he began to move forward in a dance, loudly humming the music.

She let him lead her and would have joined him in humming, but she didn't know the tune.

He twirled her, bent her over, and then brought her back up. He was smiling brightly, his eyes alight with his own enjoyment of the moment.

This was the kind of man she liked—one who was spontaneous, who danced with her on a whim, who didn't care what anyone else thought, and who appreciated the joys of life. Unlike Grady, who never did anything without first calculating every risk and hardly ever took the time to enjoy the simple things of life.

As John twirled her a final time, she laughed with pleasure . . . until he wrapped his arm around her waist and drew her abruptly against him so their bodies were pressing together.

His expression turned earnest, and desire flared in his eyes. She'd seen desire enough times over the years to be able to recognize it.

She liked having fun with young people her age, including the fellows, but *fun* was as far as she was willing to go.

She jerked her hand from John's and pushed his chest.

He only gathered her closer. "You're so beautiful, Clementine."

"Let go of me." She shoved again.

He dipped his head near hers as though he meant to kiss her.

She lifted her hand to cover his mouth. "Stop right there, mister." She wasn't opposed to kissing, but not like this and not with him.

To the side, she saw Willa halt her conversation, likely sensing the growing tension.

John broke free from her hand over his mouth. "Please, Clementine. I'd like you to be mine."

At his words—identical to what had been on the note she'd found in her coat pocket—she froze. Was John the person who'd been leaving the gifts and notes?

"Stop." She managed the one word even as her blood turned to ice. If he'd been sneaking around the store and her workroom, then he'd definitely taken things too far, and she had to make him understand the need to stop.

"I want to marry you," he continued, his voice radiating with passion.

"No, John." She struggled against him, but he refused to release her. "I'm not interested—"

He reached for her again, dragging her against his chest.

In the next instant, he was being wrenched backward and away from her. He squawked a girlish scream and flailed his arms as he strained to see what was happening.

Clementine could see easily enough. Grady had a fistful of John's coat and had lifted him off the ground by at least an inch. Grady hauled the fellow away, then flung him like dirty water being emptied from a wash basin.

John stumbled backward several steps and then toppled to his backside, landing with a hard *oomph* on the ice.

Grady was scowling fiercely. His bare arms were taut and his hockey stick raised as he stepped after John and towered above him.

"Don't touch Clementine." Grady growled out the words. On the ice, the game had come to a halt, likely because Grady had stepped out of position to be a hero she didn't need. And now all the players were watching him.

Of course she was grateful Grady was looking out for her. She wasn't naïve enough to think she could overcome a big man like John if he decided to force himself on her.

But she didn't like it when Grady ran to her rescue as though she were a damsel in distress.

"I don't know who you are," Grady was saying in a deadly tone, "but I'd better not see you anywhere near Clementine ever again."

John scooted back on the ice several inches, as if he was afraid Grady might hit him with the hockey stick. "I was just proposing—"

"Looks like she said no." Grady lowered the hockey stick, then pretended to swipe it at John.

John ducked his head and emitted another high-pitched scream.

Clementine shook her head, unable to rein in her exasperation. "Grady Worth, leave the poor fellow alone."

Grady halted the hockey stick near John's head.

Clementine strode over to Grady, huffed, then jerked the stick out of his hand.

Grady didn't spare her a glance—was too busy trying to scare John.

She wrapped a hand around Grady's arm and began to drag him away from John and away from the pond. Thankfully, he followed her, walking as easily on his ice skates as he did in his work boots. She could feel his resistance in his arm flexing beneath her fingers, the muscles hard but his skin warmer than she'd expected on the cold night.

When she reached the dark shadows that were

untouched by lantern light, she halted and spun to face him. She didn't really care if people heard her chewing Grady out, but she wanted to get him away from John so the whole incident could end without anyone getting hurt.

It wasn't the first time Grady had stepped in to try to protect her from a man getting too frisky. He'd done so on other occasions over the past few years. But the last couple of times he'd intervened, he'd given the fellows bruises—*souvenirs*, he'd said with a smirk.

"I didn't need your help, Grady." She tried to put her hands on her hips, but since she was still holding Grady's hockey stick, she could only fist one and suspected she looked only halfway peeved.

"He was about to kiss you," Grady hissed, tossing a glare at John, who was slipping and sliding and nearly falling as he tried to get off the ice and back onto solid ground.

"I realize that. And I wasn't planning to let him. I had things under control."

"It didn't look that way to me."

"Well, I did."

He rolled his eyes in typical Grady fashion. "Why can't you just stay away from the fellows, Clementine?"

She rolled her eyes too. It was immature, she knew. But sometimes she couldn't seem to help herself around Grady. He made her so mad. "Oh, so now I'm supposed to go to Denver and join a convent and become a nun?"

"Maybe." Grady leaned down so his face was a handspan away. "If that would keep you from flirting with every fellow that walks into Summit County, then maybe I'll drive you down to Denver myself."

"I'm not flirting with every fellow."

"It looks that way to me."

Clearly he'd been keeping half an eye on her while playing his game. Or perhaps he'd noticed John's advances during a break in the game's action. Whatever the case, she didn't need Grady scaring men away.

"What if I'd been planning to accept John's proposal?" She never would, but Grady hadn't known that.

Grady released a low scoff. "That pancake?"

She bit back a smile. John was a bit of a pancake, whatever that meant. Especially if he was the one secretly leaving her the gifts and notes. She still needed to tell him to stop. But maybe now, after Grady's scare tactics, she wouldn't need to.

She lifted her shoulders, then pinned him with a glare. "Stop interfering with my social life, Grady."

"Then stop being so careless with men. One of these days, all your flirting will get you into trouble."

Another denial pushed to the tip of her tongue, but Grady lifted a finger to her lips and silenced her in one touch. His finger was hard like his expression, but that hardness sent a strange shimmer along every nerve ending, all the way to her toes.

Grady's gaze dropped to his finger against her lips, and his dark eyes widened a fraction before he jerked his hand away, almost as if the touch had burned him. Then his brows furrowed into another deep scowl.

There was the Grady she knew. The grumpy pest.

From the pond, Grady's teammates were calling him to return to the game.

Grady gave them a curt nod before glowering at John and his friends, now hurrying along the path that led toward town. He watched them for a moment before taking his hockey stick from her.

"Wait for me"—his voice was much too bossy—"and I'll walk you home."

Did he think John would be in the shadows, waiting for her to pass, ready to jump out and grab her? She scoffed. "I've been walking back and forth alone all week."

"Clementine Oakley," he growled with impossibly dark eyes. "You're the most aggravating girl I know."

"Woman."

He didn't respond.

"Aggravating woman." She wasn't a girl anymore, and it was past time for him to accept it.

He sighed, then turned away and started back to the pond. "Either wait for me to walk with you, or make sure you go with Willa."

She hesitated several beats. "Fine."

As soon as she gave her answer, he picked up his pace into a jog. And a moment later he was racing on the ice as though he was trying to outrun a demon. But even with his speed, he had a control and deliberateness that never failed to amaze her.

He was a man of so many contradictions that he sometimes left her dizzy. One minute he was beating an overzealous fellow away from her with a hockey stick, and the next he acted like she was the most troublesome person he'd ever met.

There was no doubt in her mind that Grady was a good man. He watched over her like an older brother would, except that he was an annoyed older brother who had little patience for her and wished she wasn't around to bother him.

She wasn't sure what had happened to cause him to feel that way, but at some point she'd done something to earn his disdain. Or maybe as they'd gotten older, she'd changed into a person he no longer liked.

Whatever the case, he made no secret of the fact that he didn't get along with her. Maybe at first she'd been hurt, and his rejection had stung, especially because she'd adored him, had even fancied herself in love with him at one point. Over time she'd come to accept that she and Grady would never be anything but at odds with each other. And that was perfectly fine with her.

4

Willa Vance.

Grady unlaced his skate and studied Clementine's friend. He didn't care that he was staring or maybe even being obnoxious about it. If he had to pick a woman to court and fall in love with, then he couldn't be shy about it.

He didn't think Dad had any love interests yet. But Dad was friendly and not bad-looking, and sometimes women came into the store and paid him attention.

Just in case his dad already had a woman he'd been thinking about, Grady couldn't afford to sit back and waste time. Which was why he needed to survey the few single women who'd come to watch the hockey game.

A couple of women on the opposite side of the pond had been eyeing him and some of the hockey players on his team. He could go over and introduce himself and find out more about them. But why bother doing that when Willa was nearby and smiling at him, clearly having noticed his attention?

Willa was fairly new to Breckenridge—had moved into town over the past year with her family, who had come up from Denver and built a hotel. She worked there with several of her siblings.

She was pretty, especially for a fellow who liked thin, small-boned women with dark hair and pale skin. He actually preferred a more curvaceous woman with fair hair and tanned skin.

His gaze shifted to where Clementine stood, animatedly talking with Buck, one of his teammates. She was shivering and hugging her arms across her body, which only served to outline her figure with all the right curves in all the right places. Her beauty was a fact, and he wasn't going to ignore it just because he didn't like her. Of course she had the prettiest fair hair of any woman he'd ever met. And her skin still contained the golden-brown hue she'd gained over the summer.

The trouble was, every other fellow was noticing Clementine as usual. And she loved it.

He knew he shouldn't care. She was old enough to be courting. But she needed to be more selective and stop leading men on. With her laughter and talkativeness and classic flirtatious smile with a wink, she was sending messages that shouldn't be sent.

If she were less friendly, then maybe fellows wouldn't

be putting their hands all over her.

The anger from a short while ago still simmered low in his gut. Of course, he'd been aware the moment the tall fellow had reached for Clementine's hand. Then the pancake had pretended to dance with her just so he could get a feel of her body and steal a kiss. It had been obvious that was what he'd been aiming for.

When Clementine had started struggling to get loose, Grady hadn't been able to hold himself back any longer. He'd done the right thing and had gone to her defense.

He wouldn't have had to, though, if she'd been more careful.

With an exasperated sigh, he finished removing his skates, tied the laces together, and draped them over his shoulder. He'd already shrugged back into his coat, which he almost never wore while playing. Now, as he made his way toward Clementine and Willa, he swiped off his knit cap and combed his fingers through his hair, which was damp with perspiration.

He could feel Willa still watching him, waiting for him to look at her again. Although he wasn't necessarily attracted to her, he needed to consider her as a potential love interest, didn't he? He'd heard of couples who hadn't been attracted to each other at first but had simply had to give love a chance to grow.

Clementine's brother Ryder was a perfect example of that. He'd put an advertisement into a newspaper for a wife. Genevieve had traveled west, and the two of them had gotten married without knowing each other. From what he'd overheard Clementine telling his dad, now Ryder and Genevieve were *madly in love* with each other—if being *madly in love* were even possible.

Grady would settle for plain and simple love or even liking.

He forced himself to shift his attention to Willa, settling on her face, which was pretty, even if it was thin and angular.

"Good game, Grady," she said as he stopped in front of her.

He shrugged. "It was all right."

Her smile widened, and her eyes seemed to brighten. "I thought you played fabulously."

He couldn't remember if he'd ever talked to Willa before. Maybe in passing. It was time to change that and get to know her better.

She watched him expectantly, as if waiting for him to answer her comment. For a second, he stood awkwardly, unsure how to start a conversation.

"It was just an okay game." Clementine waved to Buck as he headed away with another fellow, then she turned her attention to Grady, narrowing her brow critically. "You had some good passes but missed too many goals."

"Only a few."

"More like a few dozen."

He snorted at her exaggeration.

She rubbed her mittened hands together. "You were definitely off your game tonight."

He narrowed his eyes back on her. "How would you know? You were too busy getting fresh with that pancake to watch my moves."

Clementine's narrow brows turned down into a V, and her hands dropped to her hips. "I was not getting fresh with John."

"You let him put his hands all over you."

"I did not." Her voice held a note of mortification.

He wasn't being fair. She'd done her best to make the pancake behave.

"John is very sweet." She tossed the words at him, as if they could justify everything that had happened. "In fact, he secretly left me two silk roses today at the store."

"Sweet or not, he's not the man for you."

"And who made you the expert on the kind of man I need?"

"It's not hard to see."

"Is that right? Then since you're so smart, why don't you enlighten me? Who is the perfect man for me?"

Willa's gaze was bouncing back and forth between him and Clementine, her smile slowly fading.

He almost slapped himself on the forehead. What was he doing? He needed to talk to Willa, not Clementine. It was just that the words always flowed easily with Clementine—sometimes too easily. But they'd known each other for a long time. And she was practically his sister, since his parents had treated Clementine so much like a daughter over the years.

Quickly, he shifted his gaze back to Willa. "May I walk you home, Willa?"

From the corner of his eye, he could see Clementine's mouth open as though she might say something. But then she closed it. Was she speechless?

He bit back a grin. She rarely was without something to say, so this moment deserved a special monument to mark the occasion. He was tempted to tell her, but instead held out the crook of his arm to Willa.

Willa's smile returned, doubling in size, and she sidled closer, slipping her hand into his arm.

He could feel Clementine watching them, her surprise tangible. After taking several steps away from her, he halted and tossed her a smirk. "Tag along, Clementine. I'll make sure you get home safely too."

Without waiting for her response, he started forward with Willa. This time, he forced himself to ask her a question. "How do you like living in Breckenridge so far?"

Thankfully, she answered the question in more detail, describing how it was so different from Denver and how she missed the city. He tried to listen, but he was also keeping one eye on Clementine as she moseyed several paces behind them. Of course, she said hello to every person they passed and stopped to chat twice, forcing him to halt with Willa and wait for her.

Even so, the walk to the Vance Hotel didn't take long, since it was on the western edge of town, a short distance from the pond. The newly constructed building seemed to glow in the darkness, with lights burning brightly in all of its large windows, revealing its freshly painted clapboards and a large balcony running across the second floor. From what Grady had heard, the hotel had an indoor bathtub, and that was drawing visitors eager for the luxury.

As he halted at the back entrance and said goodnight to Willa, she smiled shyly up at him.

Clementine waited a short distance away and was already chatting with a fellow who was lingering at the side of the hotel and smoking a cigar. Why couldn't she ever pass by a man without talking to him?

"Would you like to go to the dance with me tomorrow night?" Willa asked. "The one being held at Inman's Lodge?"

He dragged his attention away from Clementine and nodded curtly at Willa. "I'll meet you there."

Her smile wavered, but she gave him a few more details about the dance, which he hardly heard through his mounting irritation with Clementine. Finally, when he and Clementine were on their way again and heading down Main Street toward the store, he swallowed another chastisement.

It wasn't his business whom she talked to. Besides, she was an outgoing and friendly person with both men and women alike. It was just the way she was, and he had to stop making more out of the interactions than was warranted.

Clementine ambled beside him on the boardwalk, not in a hurry. "I didn't realize you were interested in Willa."

He wasn't all that interested, but he was planning to go to the dance with her and at least make room for something to develop between them. "She's a nice girl."

"Woman."

"You know what I mean, Clementine. You don't have to correct me."

"I'm not a girl, and neither is Willa." Her voice took on a sassy note. "And maybe it's time for you to finally start to realize it."

"What's that supposed to mean?"

Across the street, two men stumbled out of a saloon, laughing boisterously. Ahead, another group of revelers was standing near a hitching post, talking loudly.

He was tempted to slide a hand to Clementine's back in a possessive gesture, not because she belonged to him but to keep the men from paying her any heed. Instead, he stuffed his hands into his coat pockets.

"Believe it or not, I'm old enough to get married, Grady."

"I realize that."

"Do you?"

Even though at times he still thought of her as the young girl in the long braids who'd spent hours in the kitchen with his mom, he wasn't blind, and he'd noticed her growing up. It had been hard not to notice, and that had always been an issue because his noticing had taken up more space in his head than he'd wanted it to.

As they neared the general store, they veered off onto the flagstone path that wound around the building. He traipsed behind her, the light from the street fading and darkness enveloping them. Even so, they made their way easily toward the metal stairway on the side of the building, which led to the second floor.

When the upstairs room had been his bedroom years ago, he'd never minded the roundabout way of getting to his room, but he didn't like that Clementine had to go outside. He'd even debated telling Dad that he'd give up his room in the house to Clementine and take the room above the store instead. But he suspected Clementine would only protest. She'd already hesitated long enough before moving to town, and he didn't want to do anything that would send her running back to the ranch.

She halted abruptly at the base of the stairs and drew in a sharp breath.

"What?" He glanced up the dozen steps to the dark windows of her room.

But she wasn't looking at the apartment. She was focused on something sitting on the bottom step. She bent and picked up the item, which appeared to be a flower of some kind.

She moved forward a few steps until she was in the alley, where the light from a nearby business joined with the moonlight to illuminate not only a fake flower but a slip of paper dangling from it.

She'd mentioned something about the fellow at the pond giving her two roses. Was this another rose from him?

She squinted as she attempted to read something written on the paper.

What was she thinking? Did she like the gesture?

At a noise from down the alley, she jumped and glanced around with rounded eyes. Her fingers began to shake, and she tossed the flower to the ground.

Grady wasted no time in picking it up and reading the message on the note: *I like watching you fix your hair.*

His mind exploded with a dozen scenarios, none of them good. "Why are you letting that pancake watch you fix your hair?"

"I'm not." Her gaze darted up and down the alley again, as if she expected someone to jump out of the shadows.

Across from them and behind the store on a slight rise was the big house his dad had built, a dim light winking in one of its windows. The back of the stable and shed bordered the alley along with the sprawling fence that hedged in the backyard.

As far as he could tell, no one was in sight.

He dropped his sights back to the note and reread it. The words were just as unsettling the second time. "Who's watching you fix your hair?" he demanded. "Is it the fellow from the pond tonight?"

"I don't know," she answered with a shaky whisper.

He examined the gaudy flower and the piece of thin string tied in a knot to the paper. "This is ridiculous."

"It's the third one today."

"Third flower or note?"

"Both."

"And were they all this creepy?" He couldn't keep his voice from rising.

"Sort of." She reached for the note, her fingers still shaking.

She was frightened.

He shoved the flower and note into his pocket and then took hold of both of her hands. "What's going on?"

She didn't jerk away from him. Instead, she leaned in closer. "I don't know."

Was someone out there even now, watching her?

Maybe if he drew her into his embrace, he'd send a

message to the fellow to back off.

Without giving himself time to think, he tugged her closer and wrapped his arms around her.

He was surprised when she melded into him. She didn't slide her arms around him, but she did lean her head against his chest.

He didn't move except to tighten his hold, wanting to reassure her that she wasn't alone and that he wouldn't let anything happen to her. He might get irritated with her often, and he might not like everything she did, but she was still like a sister to him.

Maybe that was why Dad had said something about loving Clementine. Grady supposed that, underneath everything else, he had brotherly affection and cared about her well-being the same way he would if she were his real sister.

But his mom hadn't been able to have any more children after him, even though she'd desperately wanted another baby or two. At the time, when he'd been just a lad, all he'd known was how despondent she was after each miscarriage. Even though she'd tried to hide the crying and the melancholy, he'd heard her sobs from her bedroom and knew she didn't want to leave her bed.

The sadness had always lingered . . . until they'd moved to Breckenridge and Mom had met Clementine. Somehow Clementine had made his mom happier than she'd ever been before and had brought sunshine to their home to replace the gloom that had been hanging over them for too many years.

Grady rested his chin on Clementine's head. They used to get along better, had enjoyed many escapades and adventures together when they were younger. But time had changed them both.

Whatever the case, he had to help her in this situation. It was the right thing to do.

A movement from an adjacent building caught his attention. He tried to shift enough to get a better view of the form, but all he could see was the outline of a leg and a shoe before the person backed up.

A strange unease shimmied up his backbone.

"Come on." He spoke gently as he wrapped his arm around her back and shifted her into the crook of his arm. "Let's get you inside."

She didn't protest as he began to guide her up the steps.

He led her the whole way, only stopping when he reached the landing and held out a hand. "Key."

"It's not locked."

"Not locked?" His ire spiked again. "Why aren't you locking your door?"

"You don't lock the door to the house."

"That's because it's just me and dad."

"And why should that make a difference?" Her voice took on an irritated note now too.

"Because it does." He wasn't planning to stand at her door and argue why she needed to lock it whether she was home or not. "Just lock it from now on."

She gave a huff, broke away from his hold, and opened the door. As she crossed the room, he remained in the doorway. Both of his parents had stressed the importance of respecting a woman's privacy as well as her reputation. And even though it was nighttime and no one would see him entering Clementine's room, he stood back.

He could hear her fumbling with a match, and then a second later a lantern on her bedside table flared to life, revealing the long rectangular space with a slanted ceiling.

A stove stood in one corner, a comfy cushioned chair in front of it along with an end table cluttered with a ball of yarn, knitting needles, and what appeared to be a half-finished scarf or blanket or something. A rug his mom had braided covered the floor near the chair, and a bed took up the opposite wall.

Clementine swept her gaze over the room and halted on the bed. She sucked in a sharp gasp and started to tremble again. Positioned against the pillows was a bouquet of the fake flowers, and they were tied together with a big red ribbon.

Grady had the strange sense someone was watching them from down in the alley. He spun and glared into the alleyway and tried to find anyone or anything unusual.

Although he couldn't see much in the darkness, he called out anyway. "Leave Clementine alone, or you'll answer to me, do you hear?"

No one replied.

He peered around for another moment before stalking inside, grabbing the flowers from the bed, then returning to the door. He hurled the flowers over the landing and down to the ground. "Take your blasted flowers and throw them in the toilet."

Again, nothing but silence met his angry call.

A tightness gripped his chest. He didn't know what was going on, but he didn't like it one bit.

Everything was fine. No one was watching her.

Clementine walked along Main Street with her basket of goodies, straightened her shoulders, and forced her lips into a smile.

Everything really was fine, wasn't it? The sunshine was warming her. The morning was beautiful. Even though the air was cool, it was fresh and crisp and clean. And she hadn't seen any more roses since last night when she'd found them on her bed.

Even so, with every step she'd made over the past couple of hours, she'd been filled with a quiet sense of dread about where she'd find the next rose.

But so far, there hadn't been any.

She was hoping that meant the secret admirer had listened to Grady's rant last night to leave her alone.

Before going, Grady had made her promise to shut her curtains and lock her door. She'd been too frightened to do her usual arguing with him, and once she was alone, she'd double- and triple-checked to make sure her door was locked. This morning, before heading down to the store, she'd also made sure her door was locked.

Apparently Grady had informed his dad about the situation, and when she'd entered the store, Mr. Worth had hovered around her, following her nearly everywhere she went. He'd cautioned her against making her usual charitable deliveries.

But today was her day of the week to visit the town's widows—Mrs. Meriwether, who was older with one grown son, and Mrs. Raleigh, who was younger and had three children. Clementine hadn't wanted to let the roses and messages scare her from living her normal life. Besides, what harm could really come from silk flowers and little pieces of paper? She just had to keep reminding herself of that.

"Good morning, Mrs. Livingston," she said as cheerfully as possible to the reverend's wife, who was crossing from the parsonage to the church. The petite young woman, attired in a modest winter coat and hat, was holding her baby bundled up in blankets. She called a friendly greeting to Clementine in return.

"Good morning, Doctor Howell." Clementine waved at the doctor emerging from his office with his leather doctor's satchel.

"Good morning, Mr. Irving," she called to the lawyer

heading up the street to his business.

With each greeting to those she passed, Grady's words from the hockey game haunted her: *"Stop being so careless with men. One of these days, all your flirting will get you into trouble."*

Was he right? Had her cavalier attitude toward potential suitors given someone the false idea that she was interested in them when she wasn't? Because the truth was, as much as she enjoyed mingling with the fellows at Mill Pond or at dances or church dinners or sing-alongs or other parties, she hadn't found any man yet that had captured her attention.

Well, maybe Franz had captured her attention at the beginning of the summer when he'd arrived in Breckenridge. She'd mostly been enamored because he was a foreigner, a professor, and a gentleman with manners, so unlike most men in Summit County.

She'd thought Franz was interested in her too. But it had turned out he'd fallen in love with Clarabelle at first sight—or so he claimed. At the time, Clementine had been hurt by the secretiveness of Clarabelle's relationship with Franz.

After she'd had time to think about everything, Clementine had realized she'd been selfish and should have helped her sister win the man she loved. Unfortunately, Clementine hadn't figured out how selfish she'd been until after Clarabelle had left the high country.

Since then, she'd written numerous letters to her twin, apologizing and asking forgiveness for all that had happened. Clarabelle had written back, sending her love and wishes for Clementine to find the same kind of love and happiness that she had.

"I haven't yet, Clarabelle," she whispered.

Even though she hadn't found the same kind of love and happiness yet, it wasn't for lack of trying. She'd been doing her best all summer and autumn to meet men and get to know them. But what if she'd been trying too hard?

Grady's warning again sifted through her mind: *"Stop being so careless with men."*

She'd obviously been careless with someone who now thought she was interested enough for him to leave roses and notes and other gifts. Who could it be?

It could be anyone, because the truth was, she could count half a dozen men she'd flirted with during just the past two weeks, not to mention the past few months.

With a sigh, she rounded a corner and started up the street toward Mrs. Meriwether's small home located on the rise along the western side of town. A lone fox stood in the middle of the road ahead, and at the sight of Clementine, it darted off between the clusters of lodgepole pines that filled the hillside between the residences.

"Clementine!" came a call from behind her on Main Street.

She halted and turned to see Grady jogging toward her, his Stetson pulled low and his long coat open, revealing his usual denims and flannel shirt—and a pair of revolvers on his hips.

"Wait up," he said.

She hadn't seen him yet that morning, which wasn't unusual since he was always up before dawn and at work in the livery, tending to the horses. Although he had hired a couple of local men to help him, he still liked to have a hand in the daily chores—at least, that's what Mr. Worth claimed.

She could admit she was grateful Grady had been with her last night when she'd found the rose on the step as well as the roses on her bed. She'd appreciated his support and his levelheadedness. And he'd hugged her . . .

That had been totally unexpected. But surprisingly, it had been nice. She'd been so overwhelmed and scared and unsure what to do, but when he'd wrapped his arms around her and held her, she'd suddenly felt safe and calm and not so alone.

Of course, he'd taken charge in typical Grady fashion, bossing her around and then throwing the roses out the door and yelling into the darkness. *"Take your blasted flowers and throw them into the toilet."*

She couldn't hold back a smile at the memory of his words.

He wasn't smiling, though, as he drew nearer. In fact,

his forehead beneath his Stetson was furrowed into a deep scowl, and his brown eyes radiated with familiar angst. "Dad told me you left by yourself." The words were accusatory.

Her smile shriveled up. "Is that a crime now?"

His jaw remained rigid. Freshly shaved, it was smooth with just the hint of a shadow. "It is until we find out who's watching you fix your hair and sending you weird notes and fake flowers."

"And as I told your dad, I can't stop living my life."

"You can stop making every fellow think you like him."

She'd already come to the same conclusion, but she wasn't about to say so to Grady—not with how arrogant his attitude was at the moment. "Thank you for your concern, Grady, but I can handle this myself now." She lifted her chin and started walking up the hill again. She only made it two steps before his fingers closed about her arm, drawing her to a halt.

"Clementine, stop." His tone was exasperated.

She jerked against him.

"I need to tell you about John—"

"C-l-ementine?" came a timid call from up the hill.

Next to the yellow boxlike one-story home that belonged to Widow Meriwether, her son Elbert stood in the side yard with a rake in hand and a pile of leaves at his feet. He wore a bowler over his bald head, but his ears and nose were red with the cold.

She guessed his age to be somewhere in his mid-twenties, although with his nearly bald head and well-rounded stomach, he looked older. He hadn't gotten married yet and still lived with his mother. He was sweet, but he was also incredibly shy and could hardly get words out past his stutter.

The only work Elbert was able to do with any measure of success was landscaping. He did a little here and there for businesses or homes in the summer months and offered shoveling services during the winter.

The widow had taken in mending since her husband's passing several years ago. Somehow she earned enough combined with Elbert's meager income to provide for the two of them, but the dear woman never had any extra, and Clementine loved delivering candy that was getting too old to sell. She always added in some of her newest creations, and last week, she'd even brought Elbert a box of his favorite candy—sugared almonds.

Now, as Elbert watched her struggle with Grady, his eyes were wide and filled with concern.

She offered him a smile. "Don't mind Grady. He's on his way back to the livery. Aren't you, Grady?"

"No, actually, I'm not."

"Of course you are." She tugged her arm to free it, but Grady didn't budge. She forced herself to keep on smiling even as she sent daggers into Grady. "You're a busy man, and I'm sure you have plenty of busy things to do."

"Finish up. I'll wait."

"I loathe you."

"You love me?"

"Loathe. There's a big difference between loathing and loving. Maybe you should learn it."

"Since you love me so much, you won't mind me waiting."

A prickle formed on the back of her neck, and she glanced around to the few houses that lined the street. Was that same someone watching her again? Maybe it was for the best if Grady was with her this morning, just until she could determine more about what was going on—especially if the news he had about John was serious.

"Fine. But I refuse to hurry." She lifted her shoulders, and this time he released her, and she resumed her trek toward the house.

Grady followed on her heels but stopped when he reached the front gate and the stone path that led to the house.

The middle-aged widow was already opening the door and greeting Clementine. She was thin with wispy, pale hair, and her shoulders were slightly hunched, likely from all the time she spent bent over her mending. Even if life had been difficult for Mrs. Meriwether over recent years, she was a genuinely caring person, never failing to ask

Clementine about her life and family and how she was doing.

As with every week, Elbert left his yard work to help unload the goodies from her basket and carry them inside. When he'd finished, she looped the basket over her arm again with the remaining items for Mrs. Raleigh and her children. Clementine chatted for several more minutes before saying her goodbyes and crossing the yard toward Grady outside the gate.

With the brim of his hat pulled low, he was peering at the town below, his jaw flexing, making the lines of his face harder and more forbidding.

"You're welcome to come to dinner next week too, Grady," Mrs. Meriwether called from the stoop where she stood, her shawl gathered over her bony shoulders.

Grady shifted his attention to the widow, his brows rising with the questions he didn't ask.

"Your father is coming on Wednesday night." A flush began to color the widow's cheeks.

"Is he now?"

"He paid me a visit last night," she said simply, as if that explained everything.

Grady nodded. Apparently, the widow's answer was enough for him.

But Clementine could only stare at Mrs. Meriwether with an open mouth. What was happening? Why had Mr. Worth visited the widow, and why was she inviting him to dinner? They weren't considering courting each other, were they?

Grady gave a pointed look at Clementine's gaping mouth.

She snapped it closed.

"Just think about it," Mrs. Meriwether called. "I'd love to get to know you better too."

"Thank you, ma'am." Grady nodded politely. "But I'll have to pass this time since I play hockey most evenings. But maybe another time."

"Sure, Grady." She smiled warmly, clearly not taking offense at his refusal. "Definitely some other time, then."

Clementine was speechless as she walked beside Grady away from the Meriwethers'. Of course, Mr. Worth could get remarried. Plenty of middle-aged people did. But she'd never pictured him as the marry-again type, never thought he'd want another woman, especially after how devoted he'd been to Mrs. Worth. Quiet and introspective, Mrs. Worth had been a ravishing, dark-haired beauty, and it had always been clear that Mr. Worth adored her.

But it had been three years since she'd succumbed to lingering pneumonia. During all of that time, Mr. Worth hadn't once shown interest in any other woman—not even in the few single women who came into the store and flirted with him from time to time.

"So, your dad," she started.

Grady snorted. "Two minutes."

"Two minutes what?"

"You could only hold back your curiosity for two minutes."

"I'm a curious person. There's nothing wrong with that."

He tipped up the brim of his hat, letting the morning sunshine touch his face. It highlighted the mirth in his eyes.

At least Grady wasn't upset about his dad's courtship efforts. Knowing how much Grady had adored his mom, Clementine had expected him to object to his dad's showing affection to anyone else.

"So you don't mind that your dad is visiting the widow?"

"No. Should I?"

"I guess not. It's just that he's never seemed interested in getting remarried before."

"We had a talk about it."

"You did?"

Grady shrugged. "He thinks it's time for both of us to find wives."

Clementine jabbed a finger into his arm. "Ah-ha! That's why you walked Willa home and agreed to go to the dance with her."

He shrugged out of her jab. "Maybe."

"It is."

Grady halted and eyed the intersection of Main Street warily. "Do you want to hear about John or not?"

A strange, unsettled feeling weighed upon her chest. She wasn't exactly sure why except that the news that both Mr. Worth and Grady were looking for wives was unexpected. Yet she'd known that Grady would get married someday. He was too good-looking to stay single forever. He would have been snatched up by some young woman already if he hadn't been so standoffish.

Would Willa be the one to finally push through his reserve and earn his love?

Clementine would be happy for her friend if that happened. She really would. Even if she and Grady hadn't seen eye to eye on many things over recent years, she couldn't deny he was still a good man with a good heart. And once he set his mind to having a relationship with a woman, he'd work hard at it, because that was just the way Grady was—determined and dedicated.

Grady quirked a brow at her, clearly waiting for her to respond to something he'd said.

She had to shake off this strange feeling. "What did you ask?"

"I came to tell you what I learned about John."

"I hope it's all good. Because he's a very nice fellow—handsome, witty, fun—"

"I don't want you talking to him again." Grady's tone turned demanding.

She'd gotten exactly the reaction from Grady she'd hoped for—although she wasn't sure why she was baiting him. And she couldn't keep from more. "Maybe I want to court him."

Grady made a frustrated noise that sounded half huff and half growl. Either way, she liked it. And when Grady spun and grabbed her arm, she liked that too—more than she wanted him to know.

"I followed John and his friends up to their mine this morning." Grady's eyes were serious and intense. "And I cornered John and made him tell me everything."

She could only imagine John's fright at having a brawny man like Grady come after him again. No doubt Grady had roughed him up, threatened him, and then tossed him aside when he was done getting the information he wanted.

"So he admitted to being my secret admirer?"

"Not exactly. But he did admit to watching you through the front window of the store on a couple of occasions."

Not that she made a practice of brushing her hair at the store. In fact, she couldn't remember ever having done so. But it was possible she'd combed her fingers through loose strands. "What did he say about the roses and notes?"

"He denied any knowledge of them. But I got the feeling he was dishonest."

"About what?"

"One of his friends finally admitted that John has a fiancée back home." Grady watched her face, as though waiting for her reaction.

What was he expecting to see? Sadness? Despair? Humiliation? Whatever it was, she refused to give him a show. She shrugged and started forward. "That's fine with me. I didn't like him all that well anyway."

"I thought he was a *very nice fellow* and that you wanted to court him." Grady fell into step beside her. Was his tone condescending?

She picked up her pace. "Go away, Grady. I don't want to talk to you anymore."

He kept stride beside her. "I don't want you spending any more time with him or any of his friends."

"Fine. I won't."

"Good."

"Now go to work and let me finish my errands." She lifted her chin and forced her feet to move even faster.

He halted, leaving her to walk along by herself. When she glanced over her shoulder a moment later, he'd crossed the street and was heading in the direction of Vance Hotel. She stumbled but hurriedly caught herself before falling.

Was he going to call on Willa already this morning?

That strange feeling pressed on her chest again. She still didn't know what it was except that it was uncomfortable. Was it jealousy? Maybe she was jealous of Willa.

Clementine shook her head. She would never begrudge her dear friend finding happiness with a fellow, even if that fellow were Grady.

What Clementine didn't understand, though, was why Grady disliked her so much but was clearly willing to allow himself to have feelings for other women. What was wrong with her? Why wasn't she as likeable, even as likeable as her twin Clarabelle?

She'd been left behind in her family as her siblings had all gotten married over the past year. Now she was being left behind with Grady and Mr. Worth, and she didn't like that at all.

She was tired of being left behind, and she had to figure out a way to do something about it.

Maybe she had to get serious about finding someone to court now too—someone she could actually marry. It wasn't as though she hadn't been trying to find the right man. She had been. But clearly she had to try harder.

6

"You look nice tonight." Grady two-stepped with Willa, one hand holding hers and the other on her shoulder blade at her back.

She was smiling up at him—had actually been smiling at him since he'd arrived an hour ago at Inman's Lodge. "Thank you, Grady. I appreciate the compliment. Again."

Blast. How many times had he told her she looked nice? He'd lost count. She did look pretty in her striped skirt and matching blouse. Her dark hair was curled in fancy ringlets, and her pale face had a flush tonight.

Maybe he kept complimenting her because he was hoping that if he told her how nice she looked, he'd convince himself to be attracted to her. Because she was pretty and sweet.

Fiddle music and foot-stomping filled the lodge along with laughter. The air was stale in the crowded room, even though the double doors were wide open and letting in the cold November air.

The lodge, made of log walls and a low ceiling, was the meeting place for social clubs, political rallies, holiday parties, and other gatherings. It didn't have many windows and was always dark inside, especially at night, even though lanterns had been lit and hung from the rafters around the large room.

Two fiddlers stood at the far side next to the dancing. On the opposite end, the dessert table was filled with cakes and pies along with coffee and lemonade. The sponsors of the dance never allowed any spirits, hoping to provide an alternative to the bawdy dance halls on Main Street, where the dancing girls and drinks attracted a rougher crowd.

Not that Grady had ever gone to the dance halls or saloons. Those places didn't appeal to him, and even if they had, his dad would have whupped him good if he'd ever even thought of taking up the pastime of drinking and womanizing.

Willa was studying his face, nibbling on her bottom lip and likely trying to figure out what to talk about next. He knew he wasn't the best conversationalist, unlike his dad, who could carry on a discussion with a barn door. Even so, he needed to make more of an effort to keep the exchanges with Willa going, and so far he hadn't done much.

If he had any hope of winning the challenge his dad

had given him last evening, then he couldn't sit back and be passive about getting to know Willa. He had to be intentional and attentive. Although he'd never had a serious relationship, he'd mingled enough to know that the early stage was awkward and uncomfortable. It took time to move beyond that.

The trouble was, he didn't have a lot of time to spare—not if he hoped to beat his dad. He never would have guessed his dad was capable of moving so fast, already visiting Mrs. Meriwether and setting up supper plans. But clearly his dad was taking the challenge seriously.

Grady needed to as well.

He shifted in the two-step for several more moves before clearing his throat. "How is business at the hotel?"

"It seems to be good." Her eyes were wide upon him and shining with an admiration that was so different from the fire that was usually in Clementine's eyes. That was because Clementine was always so passionate about everything—and, okay, yes, mad at him half the time.

Regardless, he never had any trouble keeping up a conversation with her. There was no pretending, no tiptoeing around, and no false compliments. He could say whatever he wanted, and she could do the same.

So far, he hadn't seen her at the dance. John and his friends weren't there either. Which was good, because he'd warned them that morning when he'd hiked up to the mine, not to come to the dance, not to go to any more hockey games, and most certainly not to be seen within shooting distance of Clementine.

He'd only had to pound one fist—into John's ribs—to emphasize how serious he was about the boundaries. Although he'd learned the truth about John's cheating ways, he wasn't convinced that John was the one leaving the flowers and notes.

"I keep really busy," Willa said with a soft laugh. "So that must mean we're doing all right."

"That's good." Her answer wasn't what he'd wanted to hear. He was interested in the details of the hotel, like how many customers they had on average, what was the revenue versus costs, and how many staff they used to maintain the day-to-day operations. Since his dad owned a couple of hotels in Georgetown, Grady was already knowledgeable about what the business entailed and had considered the option of building a hotel in Breckenridge, especially if the population continued to increase.

But he couldn't ask Willa business questions. He needed to be more practical. "What kinds of things do you do each day?" That was a topic that would get her talking, wasn't it?

Willa moved her fingers against his. They were so thin and delicate and tentative. "I help make and serve breakfast to our guests."

He nodded, but his attention caught upon

Clementine entering through the open double doors. She was radiating with life and vibrancy, especially as she shared laughter with the young man whose arm she held.

She was attired in the dark-green skirt and bodice she'd worn before, but for some reason, tonight the hue was brighter and made the red highlights in her loose blond hair shimmer and the green of her eyes sparkle like jewels.

She seemed to be hanging on to every word from her escort. And she was hanging on to him literally, both of her hands wrapped through his arm and her shoulder pressed against his.

It was Jeremy Usher, the blacksmith's assistant. He was swaggering beside her, peering down at her with an enormous grin, as if he'd just struck a mother lode. He must have been saying something witty, because her laughter rang out above the din of everything and everyone else.

Or maybe the noise level had dropped, because most people had stopped talking to take in Clementine. How could they not be drawn to look at her with how striking she was?

But why had she come with Jeremy, who was nothing more than an overgrown child? Since the blacksmith's shop was next to the livery, Grady saw more of Jeremy every day than he wanted to. While Jeremy was a strong fellow who worked hard, he was also loud, obnoxious, and hardly ever serious about anything.

As the two began hanging their coats on the already overflowing coat tree, Jeremy pointed a finger at one of his friends and yelled a greeting. Another one of Jeremy's friends stepped away from the dance floor and shoulder-bumped Jeremy, all the while keeping his eyes on Clementine.

In return, she gave the friend one of her flirtatious smiles.

Grady's gut began to churn. This was bad. She was drawing lots of attention.

He glanced around at the faces of the other young men. If the fellow who'd sent her the roses was here, what would he think of her tonight? What if that fellow was Jeremy Usher?

Grady had absolutely no evidence that would implicate Jeremy, but at this point, every man Clementine associated with was a suspect.

"Should we go talk to Clementine?" Willa's question penetrated through Grady's racing thoughts.

Only then did he realize he'd stopped dancing, released Willa, and taken a step away from her. She was peering at Clementine hesitantly, as if she didn't really want to mingle with her friend.

"No." He didn't want to talk to Clementine or look at her. He needed to pretend she didn't exist and enjoy the rest of his evening with Willa.

But as he reached for Willa's hand again, Clementine's laughter wafted across the distance and coiled around his chest, squeezing it tight. She probably shouldn't have come. But now that she was here, she needed to be quieter and subtler, and she definitely shouldn't be flirting with every man who approached her.

With a frustrated sigh, he took hold of Willa and started to dance again. Her bright smile was gone, and a timid one had taken its place—one that said she wasn't sure what was going on anymore.

He wasn't sure what was going on either, except that his frustrations and worries about Clementine were swirling in their own two-step. He couldn't let her presence ruin his night. He had to take control of himself and the situation.

Steeling his back, he forced a smile for Willa—or at least as much of one as he could muster. Then he began dancing again, trying to ignore Clementine only a dozen paces away. But somehow, as usual, his body was attuned to every move she made, just as it had been at the hockey game last night.

He wished he weren't so aware of her. And he wished his thoughts wouldn't stray to her so often. But that was how it had always been with her, even when they'd been friends, and he supposed the habit was just too hard to break after so many years.

Even though she'd come with Jeremy, she danced

with several of his friends, laughing and gushing over them as if they were circus stars. By the time she'd finished with her third dance partner, Grady's gut was a tangle of tight knots. When she stepped away, she happened to glance Grady's way, where he was still attempting to dance with Willa and make small talk, although he wasn't doing a good job of either if her growing frown was any indication.

His gaze snagged with Clementine's, and she raised her brows to question why he was watching her. He lifted his in return, asking why she was looking at him.

She tilted up her chin and nose, denying she had any interest in him and Willa and their dancing.

He smirked, knowing full well his little half smile irritated her to no end. Then he twirled Willa and drew her closer. Not too close but enough to show Clementine he was enjoying the dance.

Her eyes narrowed just slightly. Then she pursed her lips together and glanced around. She found Jeremy, who was standing by the dessert tables and joking with one of his friends. She wound her way through the crowd, grabbed his arm, and began to drag him back to the dancing. Once there, she wrapped both arms around his neck, stood on her toes, and brushed a kiss to his mouth.

The touch was only for half a second. Maybe not even that. Either way, it was too long.

Grady halted abruptly, a shot of anger stiffening his

muscles. What was Clementine doing?

She darted a look his way, then smirked back.

Was she going around kissing fellows just to spite him? That was ridiculous. Someone had to make her come to her senses.

And that someone had to be him.

"Excuse me, Willa." Without even looking at Willa, he let go of her and stalked toward Clementine, not caring that he was bumping people out of his way.

Her back was turned to him, but he had a full view of Jeremy, who was grinning and starting to wrap his arms around Clementine in return, his eyes wide and filled with desire. He was probably planning to kiss Clementine back and wouldn't resort to a half-second peck. No, the fellow would take advantage of the situation and get in a big, long kiss.

Grady could feel a growl forming deep in his chest, and with the last two strides, he lunged for Clementine. Grabbing hold of her waist, he wrenched her out of Jeremy's arms.

Clementine released a surprised screech.

Grady dragged her back several steps, not caring what anyone else thought of what he was doing.

As she twisted in his hold, she began to wriggle to free herself. "Grady Worth, you let go of me this instant."

"No way. You're going home."

"I am not."

"Oh yes you are."

"You're not in charge of me, Grady, even though you think you are." She wrenched against him and almost broke free.

He repositioned his hands on her hips, then did the first thing that came to mind. He picked her up and slung her over his shoulder.

She released a startled scream.

He clamped his arm over her legs, dangling down his chest, and then headed toward the door.

"What do you think you're doing?" She pounded a fist against his back. "Put me down!"

He didn't answer, just strode through the crowd, which was thankfully parting on both sides, giving him plenty of room to make his escape. The music had come to an abrupt halt, and the chatter in the room was fading. He could sense all eyes upon them, and he knew he was causing a commotion.

But causing a commotion this way was better than letting her make a scene with Jeremy. With another kiss.

She slapped his back again. "You're a brute. Do you know that? A pompous, rude brute."

He honestly didn't care if he was being a brute. He was too mad to care.

With a heavy stride, he pushed past the last of the dancers and out the door. A lantern hung from a metal lamppost beside the sprawling log structure, casting a warm glow over the front yard with a stone patio and benches on either side.

A couple was sitting on the bench and appeared to be kissing. At the sight—and sound—of his stomping approach with Clementine, the young couple jumped up and separated quickly, then peered up into the sky as if they'd been doing nothing more than stargazing.

Grady didn't give them more than a cursory glance, not with Clementine ranting even louder with each step he took. As she tried to slide down, he held on tighter even as he wished he'd brought a wagon so he could toss her in the back, tie her up, and take her home.

But as he reached the rows of wagons and horses and hitching posts, he slowed down. The rage that had reared up inside him seemed to be slowing as well, allowing for a slight window of sanity.

He was breathing hard, although he wasn't sure why, because he hadn't exerted himself all that much—no more than he did when he was on the ice. Clearly he'd gotten worked up in his anger and frustration. But he was only taking care of Clementine the way he'd promised his mom before she'd died. That's all this whole situation was—his making sure Clementine stayed out of trouble.

He stepped between two wagons and finally stopped. Now that he was away from the lodge and all the light, the darkness of the night circled around him, giving him some privacy.

"You're in big trouble, Grady," Clementine said, her voice muffled behind him. She'd ceased her pounding and wriggling and now lay still across his shoulder.

Only then did he realize where his arm was holding her. Across the back of her thighs and brushing against her hindquarter. A well-rounded and firm hindquarter.

A surge of heat pumped through his gut—heat that was rising in temperature because of her proximity and her womanliness. He didn't want to think about her that way, didn't want to be affected by her allure the way other men were, didn't want to have any longings for her at all. But there was no denying the burning in his veins.

He had to put her down. Now. Before he thought about the rest of her body pressed over his shoulder and against his back.

Carefully, so that he didn't let himself feel any more of her, he set her on her feet.

The moment she was standing and her arms were free, she lifted a hand to smack him across the face.

His reflexes were quick from hockey, and he captured her wrist before she could connect with his cheek.

Even though they had only the faint light from Inman's Lodge around them, he could see the fury in her eyes and in the tight lines of her expression. "How dare you?" she hissed.

"I had every right to protect you." His whisper was cantankerous, but he didn't care.

"Protect me from what? A kiss?" Her whisper rose. "Well, thank you for rescuing me. I was in so much danger from that kiss."

He released a soft scoff. "That wasn't a kiss."

"It most certainly was." She pushed her pointer finger into his chest. "It was a good kiss."

"You obviously don't know what a good kiss is."

"And you do?"

"Of course."

"You're so arrogant."

Somehow during their arguing, they'd ended up mere inches apart, and he was still holding her wrist. Her face was upturned, her cheeks flushed, and her hair mussed. Why did she have to be so blasted pretty, even when she was angry?

Her finger on his sternum lightened, then her palm came to rest against him. Her gaze swept around his face and landed on his mouth.

Why was she looking at his mouth?

That same heat from moments ago pulsed into his blood. "It's not arrogant to state a fact."

"And what fact is that?" She was still studying his mouth.

"The fact that I'm a good kisser." He needed to tell her to stop looking at him that way. It was making him think things he shouldn't. Like what it would feel like to have her lips against his.

Her gaze shifted to his. Even though the fury was simmering there from before, something else was there too. Was it interest?

He quirked his brow. Did she want him to show her how he kissed?

As though sensing his question, or maybe seeing the rise of his brow, she scoffed and started to push at his chest.

He grabbed her wrist on that hand too, so he was now gripping both wrists and holding her in place. "Guess now's as good a time as any to prove that I'm right."

"Or wrong." She didn't try to pull away. Instead, she seemed to be waiting. "You're almost always wrong."

"You know I'm almost always right." His gaze fell to her lips as if drawn there by a power he couldn't resist. The second he let himself look at her pretty, sassy lips, all he could do was bend in and take those pretty, sassy lips with his.

As his lips touched hers, her lashes dropped, and she released a surprised gasp that he captured hungrily. His hands slid from her wrists up her arms. In the next second, her fingers clutched at his shirt as though she needed to keep from sinking down. Then she twisted his shirt and jerked him nearer.

The jerk seemed to loosen something inside him. He could only describe it as raw need. Not need for just any woman. No, this need was for only her. And it coursed through him with a strength that left him breathless.

As he fused his mouth more deeply with hers, she didn't seem to know quite how to respond. And for a reason he couldn't explain, he was relieved that she wasn't practiced at kissing—at least, beyond anything quick and chaste. Even if she flirted all the time, she'd been smart enough to set boundaries.

It was a good thing. Because just one taste of her lips would make any man a goner.

Those lips had a softness that was both pliable and firm—just like her, sweet at times and frustrating at others. As she finally caught on to meshing her lips with his and started kissing him back, the eagerness of her mouth against his sent a fresh burst of flames through his body, setting him on fire.

He didn't want to feel this kind of need for her, didn't want to desire her, didn't want to kiss her. But when she rose into the kiss even more fully and began to stir against him with a clear need of her own, he forced back a groan of pleasure.

He'd never expected to be kissing Clementine, the woman who was a thorn in his side. And he'd most certainly never expected it to be like this.

7

Heaven have mercy on her poor soul.

Grady Worth hadn't been lying. He was a good kisser. In fact, he was an expert. Not that she had much to compare his kisses to in her very short history of kissing men. Like Jeremy.

Grady had been right. The kiss with Jeremy hadn't really been a kiss.

Clementine let her lips blend with Grady's again and again with a rhythm that was growing only faster and more desperate. Desperate for what, she didn't know. But she could feel herself heating, her skin flushing, her body keening for him.

If she kept going, he was only going to gloat all the more that he'd been right. He would be insufferable. But there was a part of her that simply didn't care. In fact, that same part of her even liked insufferable Grady when he cocked his brow at her and gave her that smirk.

Especially when he had messy hair after a hockey game and a day's worth of scruff.

Not that he didn't look appealing tonight too, all cleaned up with his hair combed and slicked back and his jaw freshly shaved. When she'd been watching him dance with Willa—which hadn't been often, or at least, not too often—his trousers had outlined his muscular thighs. He'd worn a vest over his white button-down shirt but had rolled the sleeves up, so his muscular arms had been on display.

The indisputable truth was that Grady was an attractive man. She couldn't deny it any more than she could deny that the sky had stars.

A throat cleared behind them.

Oh dear Lord. What was she doing kissing Grady? She couldn't—shouldn't be. Not for any reason at all. And he shouldn't be kissing her either.

But his lips seemed to be giving her a message all of their own—one that said he wanted to keep kissing her, that he was enjoying the moment as much as she was.

The throat cleared again, more loudly. "I should have seen this coming a mile away."

Willa?

Clementine broke from the kiss. She shoved Grady behind herself as though she could make him disappear. Willa stood several paces away, hands on her hips and her eyes brimming with hurt.

Clementine tried to draw in a steadying breath, but she couldn't manage past the rapid rising and falling of her chest. She held out a hand toward Willa, but it was shaking, so she hid it behind her back.

"Willa, what are you doing out here?" The question was silly, and the moment she spoke it, she wished she could take it back.

Willa's gaze darted past Clementine to Grady. "I wanted to make sure everything was okay."

"I'm sorry, Willa." Grady's voice held contrition, and he stepped around Clementine, clearly unwilling to just go away and disappear the way she would have preferred. "I was wrong to come out here and kiss Clementine. I didn't mean for it to happen. It shouldn't have happened."

The anger in Willa's expression fell away as she searched Grady's face. What did she hope to see there?

Clementine glanced sideways at Grady.

His jaw was hard and his lips set firmly—those lips that only seconds ago had been pressed against hers as if that was where they were meant to be.

Delicious heat radiated through her abdomen. But she couldn't allow herself to feel that heat. And she couldn't allow herself to look at his lips. Never again.

Though he was offering an apology, his shoulders were rigid and his expression tense. "I'm leaving the dance now."

Willa's shoulders slumped. No doubt she'd had higher hopes for the evening, had probably expected Grady to stay until the end and then walk her home and maybe even give her a goodnight kiss. And now her dreams had been dashed.

"I'm sorry too." Clementine hadn't been thinking of her friend when she'd kissed Grady. That had been selfish, inconsiderate, and downright mean. "I was totally insensitive to you—"

"Don't." Willa held up a hand.

Clementine knew there were no excuses for what she'd done. She'd been wrong to kiss Grady, and now she'd hurt her friend. "It didn't mean anything. Grady doesn't mean anything. Everyone knows we fight all the time."

Beside her, Grady stiffened, but he didn't deny her statements.

Willa released a humorless laugh. "Everyone knows the reason you fight all the time is because you like each other."

"That's not true. We can't stand each other."

"You can't stand to watch each other with someone else." Willa's tone was laced with pain and anger. "You didn't like that Grady is with me, so you had to flaunt bringing Jeremy."

Clementine didn't blame her friend for being upset. But she wasn't right about Jeremy, was she? A nagging at the back of her mind told her that Willa was at least partially correct—at least about showing off Jeremy.

She'd stewed all day over Grady's revelation that he and his dad intended to start courting. By the afternoon, she'd been about to burst with the frustration inside. So when Jeremy had walked in to buy his daily piece of candy, she'd asked him to go to the dance with her. She'd decided maybe she hadn't given him enough serious consideration yet. She'd thought spending the evening with him would allow her to get to know him better so that feelings could develop.

But she'd only needed the walk to the lodge to confirm that feelings would never develop with Jeremy. Maybe she'd even already known that but had hoped she was wrong.

Whatever the case, she was back to the same place she'd been in earlier in the day. She was being left behind again.

Had she kissed Grady to sabotage his courtship so he wouldn't get further ahead of her in a relationship? Yes, that had to be why. It certainly wasn't because she was attracted to him the way Willa was insinuating.

Clementine opened her mouth to explain more, but her friend cut her off with a curt shake of her head. "Don't say anything else, Clem. You could have any other fellow in town. Why couldn't you let me have just one?"

Clementine bit back a sigh along with the

explanation. There really was nothing that could excuse how selfish she'd been. "I'm sorry—"

"And don't apologize again either." Willa's stricken gaze cut into her. "There's no apology that can make up for it."

With that, Willa spun and began to stride toward the lodge. Jeremy was standing just outside the door, watching them, his hands shoved into his pockets and his shoulders slumped.

Had he seen her kissing Grady too?

As Willa approached, he straightened and spoke quietly to her. She nodded in response. He held out his arm to her, and she only hesitated a moment before slipping her hand into the crook of his elbow and allowing him to escort her inside.

Clementine stared after the couple and crossed her fingers that Willa wouldn't be hurt for too long, that maybe she'd end up having a better time with Jeremy. After all, Grady wasn't right for her.

She wasn't sure how she knew that, only that she did. Maybe it was because as handsome as Grady was, he was gruff and blunt and wouldn't be right for many women. He would need someone special to put up with him.

"Let's go." He spoke beside her, and his voice held a finality that irked her.

"What if I'm not ready to go yet?"

His expression was severe as he took hold of her arm.

"Don't make me throw you over my shoulder again."

She huffed and pulled away from him. "You wouldn't."

"Try me."

She glanced toward the lodge's open door. Jeremy and Willa had disappeared inside, and a different couple stepped past in a twirling dance move. The lively tune of the current selection wafted outside.

She really had no desire to rejoin the festivities—not after all that had just happened with Willa and with Grady. She was still breathless after sharing the kiss with him. How would she be able to keep dancing and pretend her whole world hadn't been tipped upside down?

Because it had. She'd just kissed Grady.

She peeked at him sideways.

He was staring off into the distance, a scowl marring his forehead. Was he thinking about their kiss? How had it affected him?

He stood silently another moment, then he started back toward the lodge. "I'll go get our coats."

"I'll go with you."

He didn't say anything until he reached the door. "Wait outside," he tossed over his shoulder as he entered.

She huffed and started to follow him through the door, but at the sight of Willa and Jeremy talking in low tones only half a dozen feet away, Willa wiping tears from her cheeks, Clementine hung back.

A heaviness pressed down on her chest. She'd hurt Willa more than she'd realized.

If only she hadn't kissed Grady. It had been a terrible lapse in judgment for both of them, and they couldn't let it happen again. Not that Grady would ever want to kiss her again. He'd made the point he'd been aiming for—to prove that she hadn't known what a real kiss was.

The kiss with her probably hadn't affected him nearly the same way it had her. No doubt he'd kissed a dozen other women in his lifetime with just as much passion and desire. He would forget all about this one with her and wouldn't think about it ever again.

She'd have to do the same. It was the only option.

A moment later, he stepped back out into the darkness, shrugging into his coat while holding on to hers. As he finished putting on his, he held hers up and began to drape it over her shoulders, clearly intending to be polite and help her into it. She wanted to grab the coat and don it by herself, but if he was being polite to her, then she ought to be polite in return. Was it a truce of sorts?

Whatever it was, she quietly let him be a gentleman.

When she finished buttoning the front, he waved her forward and then fell into step beside her.

"I can walk home by myself, you know."

"No." The single word was testy.

For a reason she couldn't explain, the return of his

grumpiness put her at ease. Maybe it was because she didn't want things to become awkward between them now that they'd kissed.

She breathed in deeply of the night air, then stuck her hands in her pockets and fished for her mittens. Something silky brushed against her fingers.

As her hand closed about an item, her steps faltered. When she pulled out a silk rose, she froze.

Two steps ahead of her, Grady halted and tossed her a narrowed look. As his sights connected with the rose she was holding out, he spun around, his eyes widening. "Did you just find that?"

She nodded, taking in the slip of paper dangling from the ribbon that was attached to the rose. She could make out the now-familiar messy handwriting but couldn't read the words in the darkness of the residential stretch of street with only a few house lanterns glowing behind curtains.

"The flower wasn't there when you arrived at the dance?" he asked.

"No." After arriving at the dance, she'd taken off her mittens and stuck them in her pocket. Nothing had been there then. "At least, I don't think so."

"That means he was at the dance." Grady peered back at Inman's Lodge, sitting at the base of a tall slope. It looked cozy and warm with the lights glowing from the windows and out the doors.

The man responsible for the roses and notes was inside. What if she'd danced next to him? What if she'd even danced with him? "Do you think Jeremy is doing this?"

Grady stared at the lodge. "I don't know. But tomorrow I'll be paying him a visit and making sure he understands never to come around you again."

"You can't do that."

"I can and will."

"Are you planning to do it for every man in Breckenridge I've ever talked to?"

"If I need to, yes." He turned his attention away from the lodge and back to the rose. "Let's find some light and see what creepy message he left this time."

They walked silently along until they reached Main Street, where the light and noise on a Friday night poured from the saloons. Grady halted in a bright spot and held the note up so they could both read it.

"You are so pretty when you sleep."

Her pulse clattered to a sickening halt. She didn't realize her legs were buckling or that she was grabbing on to Grady until his arm slid behind her back and caught her.

"Grady," she whispered, her voice strangled by sudden fear. "Do you think he's really watched me . . ." She couldn't even finish the sentence. The prospect of anyone invading her privacy enough to spy on her while she was sleeping was too mortifying to even put into words.

Grady glanced at the men loitering on Main Street, mostly around the saloon doors and some exiting a dance hall down the street. His dark eyes had turned lethal, as if he intended to kill someone right then and there.

Did his reaction mean it was possible someone had stood outside the lone window at the top of the stairs and peeked through a slit in her curtain as she'd slept? But how would the fellow have been able to see through the darkness . . . unless he'd come inside her apartment while she'd been asleep?

The sickening feeling swelled, and she clamped a hand over her mouth to keep the nausea from rising any further.

"This is getting out of hand," Grady growled as he began to guide her forward. "You're staying with me and Dad in the house tonight."

She nodded but could hardly concentrate on what he was saying since her mind was racing with the prospect that someone had entered her room while she'd been there, and she hadn't known it.

How close had the intruder stood? And how long had he watched her sleep?

She shuddered.

"This fruitcake is taking things too far." Grady picked up his pace, nearly carrying her along since she was too distracted and frightened to keep track of where she was going.

"I don't understand why anyone would want to watch me sleep."

"The same reason he was watching you fix your hair."

"Why?" The one word contained all her distress as tears threatened at the backs of her eyes.

"Because he's obsessed with you."

"I don't know anyone like that."

"That's because you're naïve."

She wanted to argue with Grady, but she was too overwhelmed to fight him. Besides, maybe he was right. Again. Why did he have to be right about so many things?

Grady directed her through a back gate from the alley, crossed the yard, and then led her through the rear door of the house and up a short staircase into the kitchen. The scent of corned beef lingered in the air, but the spacious room was dark. Even so, she knew where everything was. She'd spent many hours there with Mrs. Worth, baking and making candy, and it felt like home almost as much as the High C Ranch kitchen.

They followed the glow of light down a hallway until they reached a room that Mr. Worth used for his study. He was sitting at his desk, bent over ledgers, and a double-globe lamp with elegant roses painted on the glass shone over neatly stacked piles of papers and books in front of him.

"How was the dance . . ." Mr. Worth glanced up through spectacles, and his eyes rounded at the sight of her with Grady.

"Hello, Clementine." He offered her a warm smile. But as he took in her face and then Grady's, his smile rapidly faded. "What happened?"

Grady tossed the rose with the note onto the open ledger in front of his dad. "Someone keeps giving Clementine fake flowers with notes. I want to find out who it is and make them stop."

Mr. Worth studied Grady's face and then seemed to take note of Grady's arm still around her.

She'd been too flustered to pay attention to his hold, but now, suddenly, she was all too aware of the solidness of his arm against her lower back and the easy way he was bracing her.

She straightened and pushed away from Grady.

Grady quickly released her, as though he hadn't realized he'd still been touching her either.

Mr. Worth's gaze bounced back and forth between them. Could he tell something was different about them? That they'd kissed? The wise storekeeper always had been able to see and know everything.

Grady folded his arms across his broad chest. "Until the flowers and notes stop, Clementine is staying in the house with us." Grady wasn't asking for his dad's permission. Instead, he was telling him, which was typical Grady style.

She frowned at him. "I don't want to impose. Maybe I should just go home to the ranch. Maverick and Hazel told me I could always move home."

Grady leveled a frown back at her. "It's too far away. If something happens, it'll take me too long to get there to help you."

"I'll have Maverick and all the ranch hands."

"And what about the ride into town every day? Who will be with you then?" Grady shook his head. "No. You'll stay here in the house, where we can keep a better eye on you."

She opened her mouth to protest.

But Mr. Worth spoke first. "I agree with Grady. This is closer to the store. I wouldn't want you riding that distance into town alone—not with someone out there stalking you."

She shivered just thinking about it.

"Then it's settled. I'll go get your things from your room." Grady was taking charge and being protective—two things he did well.

Her mind jumped back to the kiss and the passion of his lips against hers. In spite of the new rose and note, the memory of his kiss—the way his lips had commanded hers so decisively, just like he was commanding this situation—still lingered on every tingling part of her lips.

Mr. Worth reclined in his chair, a satisfied gleam in his eyes. "Grady, put Clementine in the room right across from yours. Then leave the doors open so you can keep an eye on her."

Grady didn't hesitate. "Good idea."

Were the two men going a tad overboard? She wasn't sure. But one thing was for certain. She wouldn't complain. At least, not tonight.

8

Grady stood at the end of the upstairs hallway and peered through the window down into the alley, his eyes fully adjusted to the darkness.

He wasn't sure what he expected to see at the midnight hour, but the truth was, he couldn't slumber. Not with his door wide open and Clementine lying in the guest room bed only a dozen steps away.

The good Lord knew he'd tried to fall asleep. He'd tried for at least an hour. But all he'd done was toss and turn while his mind endlessly replayed the kiss with her.

And the good Lord knew he'd tried to keep from thinking about that kiss too, but he couldn't think about anything else. He'd thought about it while going back over to her apartment to gather the clothing and other items she needed. He'd thought about it while showing her upstairs to her room. He'd thought about it when she'd turned out her light and said goodnight.

Even now, as he stood silent as a sentry, his mind was filled with the kiss.

He released a tight sigh that did nothing to release the tension in his body. He shouldn't have looked at her in the bed. It had only made things worse.

She'd been lying on her side facing the door, which had given him a clear view of her in her nightgown with her long hair unbound and flowing all around her. The irritation and frustration that often lined her features had been gone. Instead, her face had been peaceful and soft, her long lashes resting against her cheeks.

He could admit, he liked this version of her. It reminded him of the friendly relationship they'd shared when they were younger, when she'd looked up at him with admiration in her eyes.

If he were really honest with himself, he knew he was the reason she'd lost her admiration, the reason why she was irritated and frustrated so much of the time. Because he'd changed. He'd grown up. And he'd let his own issues—anger and pettiness—crowd her out of his life.

What had caused his anger and pettiness? He couldn't remember anymore. But he did know she hadn't done anything to cause him to be angry. Or at least, not directly.

He started to lean against the wall, but at a movement in the shadows down in the alley, he tensed and stared at the spot carefully.

Had he actually seen someone slinking around behind the store? Or was it a wild creature trying to get into a trash bin?

He scanned the area, hoping he was hidden enough behind the curtain that, if someone was out there, they wouldn't be able to see him watching the back of the store and the side stairway that led to the upstairs room.

The note from earlier had disturbed him more than he'd admitted to Clementine or even his dad. He hated the thought that a man had crept into her room while she was asleep and unaware of the danger.

At the thought of what could have happened, his heartbeat stumbled again, just as it had when he'd read the note the first time. Thankfully, the stranger hadn't harmed Clementine in any way.

But what would he try the next time?

Grady didn't even want to think about it. If he had his way, he'd lock Clementine in the house until they figured out who was leaving her the notes. But he couldn't cage her away forever. And he couldn't stay awake every night, staring out the window and waiting for her secret admirer to show himself.

So what should he do?

"Grady?" came her sleepy voice behind him.

He shifted away from the window to find her standing in the hallway just outside the guest room. Although the darkness mostly shrouded her, he could see her slender frame in the moonlight that illuminated the night. Her hair tumbled over her nightgown, falling nearly to her waist, her arms hugged her chest, and her bare feet poked out from underneath the hem.

"What's wrong?" she asked.

Everything was wrong, including the fact that she was in his house at night, standing only a few feet away and looking bed-tousled.

He didn't want the heat from earlier to fan to life again, but it did anyway. This time it was a slow burning that began to pulse through his blood.

She rubbed at her eyes, then glanced to the window. "Is someone outside?"

"It's nothing to worry about."

She started to cross to him and the window, too stubborn to take his word on the matter.

"No, Clementine." He held out a hand to stop her.

"I have a right to know if I'm in danger."

"You'll be in danger from me if you don't stop."

She scoffed. "I doubt that."

He stepped more fully in front of the windows, guessing that if an intruder in the alley hadn't known he was there, they would now. "Go back to bed."

She halted mere inches away and smelled pretty, like flowers—probably the soap he'd brought over with her other toiletries. "If you don't have to go to bed, why do I?"

He didn't want to explain to her why he was awake at the late hour—that it was because of his worry over her as well as his runaway thoughts of their kiss. He didn't want to give her the satisfaction of knowing she could unravel him so easily.

And why, exactly, was he letting her unravel him?

He stiffened his shoulders. He was acting like a besotted fool, and he had to put an end to the rapidly mounting attraction before it gained too much power over him.

"Do you ever listen?" He let testiness infuse his tone.

"When it suits me."

It was his turn to scoff. "Maybe if you'd learned to listen, you wouldn't be in this situation."

She dropped a fist to her waist, which only served to highlight the curve of her hip beneath the nightgown. "Are you saying this is all my fault?"

"I've warned you to stop flirting, that it would get you into trouble. And now here we are."

Her nightgown was slipping down one shoulder, leaving a bare patch of skin exposed. His fingers tensed with the need to graze that spot, to test how soft it was, to feel her shiver with pleasure.

Not that she would shiver with pleasure with him. Not when she could hardly stand being around him half the time.

Even so, she'd kissed him back, which meant she

must have felt some of the same attraction he'd felt. What would she think if he bent down, brushed aside her hair, and kissed that curve in her shoulder? Would she push him away?

He growled at himself and then gave a curt shake of his head. She was too beautiful standing there all fiery and provoked, and he needed her to go back to her room, crawl into bed, and stay far away from him.

In fact, he had to say something that would put the barriers back up between them so that he would stop thinking of her as someone desirable. "As far as I'm concerned, you need to stop trying so hard with fellows. It makes you look desperate."

She stiffened. "Desperate?"

"You know what I think?"

"No. I don't care—"

"I think you're trying so hard because you can't stand that Clarabelle is married and you aren't."

Her expression turned icy. "You think you know everything, don't you?"

"I'm right this time." Talking about Clarabelle was an easy way to push Clementine away. She was sensitive about her twin and always had been, and she would stomp off in a matter of seconds.

"You're arrogant and self-absorbed." She retreated a step. "And I don't like you."

"Oh, you like me. And that's why you came out here

into the hallway. Because you wanted to kiss me again." There. If she wasn't already mad enough, she would be livid now.

"Kiss you again?" Her tone rose, no longer a whisper.

His dad slept in the bedroom downstairs, but in the silence of the night, no doubt he would hear their argument if he were awake. He'd heard plenty of their disagreements in the past, but Grady prayed he'd stay asleep and oblivious to this particular conversation.

"I regret kissing you the first time." She fairly spat her declaration. "And I would never kiss you again, not even if someone tried to force me at gunpoint."

Without waiting for his response, she spun and stomped down the hallway and disappeared into her room. A couple of seconds later, the mattress and bedsprings squeaked, signaling that she was getting back into bed.

Only after the squeaking stopped did he allow himself to breathe freely. Even then, he remained in the same spot, afraid that if he moved, he'd chase after her and tell her he was the one who wanted another kiss.

Because no matter how much he might deny it, now that he'd gotten a taste of her lips, he was hungry for more.

Someone was following her.

Clementine picked up her pace as she hurried down the side street, away from the Vance Hotel. She'd wanted to do something to apologize to Willa after the horrible end to the dance last night, so she'd put together a package with Willa's favorite candies and rushed over to deliver it to her friend first thing this morning.

Willa had been busy helping serve breakfast to the hotel's patrons, her hands full of platters and bowls as she rushed in and out of the kitchen. She'd barely stopped to acknowledge Clementine's presence, much less look inside the basket at the peace offering.

The visit hadn't restored her to Willa's good graces. Maybe nothing ever would. And maybe she'd lost a friend. The very thought brought a sting of tears to her eyes.

At the scuff of nearby footsteps, she blinked back the

tears and glanced behind herself at the row of newly built businesses, including the one belonging to the newspaper, where Milton Fogg worked. What if he'd spotted her passing by a short while ago and decided to come out and talk to her?

Her mind had been sorting through all the options for who had left the rose and note inside her coat pocket last night. Milton had been at the dance. It could have been him. He'd been watching her at one point. Had he been jealous?

Whether Milton or another man, she suspected that the fellow was out this morning and trailing her.

Clementine paused. So did the slap of footsteps. As she resumed, so did the steps.

Yes, someone was definitely following her. But in the bright morning sunshine, what did she have to fear? He wouldn't try anything in the daylight, would he? Especially on a busy Saturday morning.

When she'd awoken at dawn to Grady already dressed and leaving his room across the hallway, she'd tried to ignore him—especially after his comments of the night before.

It was probably a good thing he'd been rude to her so that she'd gone running back to her bed and away from him as quickly as possible, because she couldn't deny that she *had* been thinking about his kiss. She'd been strangely charged, wanting to be with him in a way she couldn't explain. Kissing him again wouldn't have been a good idea, especially since they'd been alone upstairs in the dark.

Not that she'd ever let anything happen with Grady. But the sleeping arrangements weren't necessarily appropriate for two single people. Of course, Mr. Worth had suggested it so Grady could protect her. The dear man probably thought he had nothing to worry about—not with the way she and Grady always fought.

Regardless, on his way to work this morning, Grady had stepped into her bedroom doorway, giving her no choice but to acknowledge his presence.

He'd warned her against going anywhere without him, had indicated she'd be safer for the time being if she had an escort. But she hadn't liked his bossiness or the way he'd assumed she would do whatever he commanded, as if he were the president of the United States of America. When he'd sauntered off without even waiting for her to respond, she'd jumped out of bed and hurried after him.

He'd already been halfway down the stairs and hadn't bothered to look back at her when she'd told him she planned to do her usual visiting and would like to see him try to stop her.

It had been childish of her, she knew. But he always seemed to draw out her worst. Now, as she hurried back in the direction of the store, she wished she had waited for someone to go with her. She could have gone later today, maybe even tonight.

She drew in a breath of cold morning air. Frost coated the rooftops of the homes and businesses on both sides of the wide street. It also covered the patches of sparse grass in a sheen of white crystals.

The western mountains of the valley, which rose up behind the town, were bathed in sunlight from the rays peeking over the eastern range. Even though the sun was making an appearance, it wouldn't be able to warm the air today. And it certainly wouldn't be able to take away the chill pulsing through her with increasing force.

If someone was after her, should she stop and confront them? That really would be the best way to find out who was behind it.

She slowed her steps, and the footsteps also slowed.

Closing her eyes briefly, she took a fortifying breath before she halted abruptly and spun. As she did so, she scanned the street, first up one side and then down the other. Several men and a few women lingered about, some chatting on the street, others walking along just as she was.

No one looked suspicious. And no one was close enough to be following her—at least, not that she could tell.

With an exasperated sigh, she turned and began to plod along again. The footsteps started up almost immediately. When she glanced over her shoulder, this time she caught a glimpse of a fellow who seemed to be trailing her, his coat collar pulled up and the brim of his derby hat tugged low to hide his face.

Although she couldn't distinguish him in one glance, there was something about his stout frame that looked familiar. And something that seemed menacing, as if he intended to grab hold of her and never let her go.

Her heart began thudding a warning to flee so that he couldn't reach her, but another part of her urged her to be brave and confront the man. If she did so, she'd know once and for all who the man was and could talk to him and make him see reason.

Bracing her shoulders, she halted and spun again. "Stop following me. And stop giving me notes. I'm not interested! Do you hear?"

But the man was already veering off the road, lunging to the side of the nearest business and disappearing from sight.

She waited for a long second for him to poke his head out and check her progress, but he didn't emerge. Was he walking down an alley? Maybe he'd be waiting at the end of the street as she passed by.

With a fresh sense of dread, she started forward, her gaze darting around as she searched for the man and prayed she would stay clear of him. As she turned onto Main Street, the open double doors of the livery seemed to beckon to her.

She picked up her skirt and started to run toward open doorway, not caring that she was drawing stares or making other pedestrians have to step out of her way. Suddenly, all that mattered was finding Grady. He'd know what to do about the person following her. Maybe they could go out together and track him down.

Her heart was thudding as hard as her footsteps as she reached the livery. A barn-like structure, the building was crowded with several wagons, a carriage, and another rig. Horse stalls lined the back part of the livery, where Grady kept fine mounts for lease and also boarded horses for those in town who didn't have a stable or barn of their own.

In the shadows near the horse stalls, Grady's ruddy-faced assistant halted his work, his eyes widening upon her. He'd been at the lodge last night, joking and laughing with Jeremy. She hadn't danced with him, but he'd always been nice to her. No doubt he'd heard what had happened with the kiss and that she'd left the dance with Grady instead of Jeremy.

As she stepped further inside, the waft of horseflesh and hay greeted her, as did the warmth radiating from the livestock. The light pouring in from the open doors revealed Grady standing next to a stranger, and they were looking at Grady's buggy. Probably a customer who wanted to rent it.

At the sight of her, Grady's conversation with the man came to an abrupt halt. Without excusing himself, Grady strode toward her across the puncheon floor strewn with straw, his expression lined with concern as he scanned her from her hat down to her boots.

"What happened?" His tone was as demanding as always.

But in that moment, she didn't care. Instead, she loved that he was dropping everything for her and that his dark eyes were radiating concern.

As Grady neared her, he reached for her arm, as though he intended to draw her even closer, but he visibly stopped himself, sticking his hands into his pockets. "Are you all right?"

She was breathing hard from racing the last of the distance to the livery, and now that she was here, she glanced outside to the street behind her, half expecting to see her pursuer standing there. "Someone was following me."

With furrowing brows, he peered out the doors. "Around the store?"

She hesitated.

"Don't tell me you went out this morning by yourself." Grady's voice dropped.

"I realize now that I shouldn't have—"

"Blast it, Clementine." His exasperated tone drew the attention of his customer and his assistant.

"I'm sorry." She hung her head. "I didn't think I would be in danger walking around town."

Grady was silent a beat. Then he nodded at his customer. "I'll be back in a few minutes. My assistant will help you until I return."

With that, Grady walked with her out of the livery. Beneath the brim of his hat, his keen gaze took in everything around them—the wagon rattling past, a young mother and children entering the store, a shopkeeper washing his front window.

She searched around too, but the man who'd been following her was nowhere in sight. "I don't see him anymore."

"Of course not. But he's still there." Grady's tone was terse as they crossed the street to the store. Once she was back inside, he leveled a stern look at her. "Next time you want to go out, you'll make sure to have someone with you?"

Her heart rate was finally beginning to slow to a normal pace. She nodded as she unwound the scarf from her neck. "I'll be more careful from now on."

"Good." With that, he began to clomp away, heading to the back, where Mr. Worth was sipping a mug of coffee and having a lively discussion with one of his friends.

As she tugged off her mittens, her attention snagged upon a silk rose on the counter behind one of her candy jars.

"Grady," she hissed as dread rushed in to crowd out her last vestiges of confidence.

He paused and tossed her a questioning glance.

She nodded at the rose.

He followed her gaze. Then with a scowl, he retraced his steps and picked up the flower. Another note dangled from it.

She hugged her arms across her chest, feeling suddenly cold even though she hadn't yet shed her coat. The rose hadn't been there when she'd left for the hotel to talk to Willa. So had the person delivered it while she'd been gone?

Maybe the person was in the store even now.

She scanned the customers for anyone who looked suspicious. Most were either women or older men, none of whom appeared particularly threatening.

Grady was already reading the note. When he finished, he held it out so she could see the message.

Hesitantly, she scanned the words. *"You're the only woman for me, and I want to marry you."*

"Oh dear." Her secret admirer was obviously very serious about her. But who was he? And why wouldn't he make himself known? What was the point of being so secretive?

"What should I do, Grady?" she whispered, this time glancing out the front window to the street, wishing she could catch someone staring inside at her. "How does he keep getting in and out of here without anyone spotting him?"

"Good question." With a firm set to his lips, he started toward his dad.

At Grady's approach, Mr. Worth's smile dimmed, and he lowered his coffee.

"I need a word with you." Grady barked the demand before disappearing past the curtain into the back of the store.

Mr. Worth raised his brow at Clementine as if to ask what he'd done to irritate Grady.

She didn't know and lifted her shoulders in apology.

Grady was a hard man to understand. Given the many years she'd known him, she should have figured him out by now. But he never failed to keep her guessing, and she supposed that was one thing she liked about him. He wasn't shallow. Instead, he was made up of deep layers with deep feelings and deep passions.

He would make some lucky woman a great husband because he would be serious and intentional and determined to make his marriage work. She wouldn't be that lucky woman, and surprisingly, she felt a twinge of jealousy toward the woman who would be.

"What were you thinking?" Grady tried to keep his voice level and low, but it rose anyway in the crowded workroom at the back of the store.

His dad plied open a crate of new merchandise. "I asked her if she could wait for you to escort her, but she said it would be awkward if you came along to visit the date you left at the dance last night."

Grady leaned a hip against the worktable where a few new batches of Clementine's candy were cooling. The waft of the sweets lingered in the air—a mixture of chocolate and nuts. "You could have gone with her."

"And leave my customers and the store untended?" His dad pulled out a stack of mittens and hats from a shipment of winter gear. "Besides, I wasn't expecting anyone to follow her around town during broad daylight."

"I'd rather err on the side of caution than let

something happen to her."

"I would too."

"Then keep a better eye on her."

"I was trying—"

"She got another note." Grady threw the newest fake flower onto the table.

Dad paused in his work and picked up the flower with the note dangling from it. As he read it, his brow furrowed. "The fellow is persistent."

"And a fruitcake if he's assuming Clementine will want to marry him after proposing to her this way."

"It is an odd way to try to woo a woman."

"Then we're agreed. You need to watch her better in the store since the deranged idiot is obviously coming inside near her."

"I'll try, son, but I get busy and can't always keep my eyes on her."

"And no more letting her go out on her own."

His dad paused in his unloading of the crate and shot him a look. "I can only do so much, Grady. Clementine is a strong-willed woman and quite the handful."

"I know that full well."

"I bet you do." His dad's voice filled with humor.

"What's that supposed to mean?"

His dad straightened, his eyes crinkling at the corners and his expression holding a happiness Grady hadn't seen there in a long time. "Lots of people are talking about last night."

"So?" Grady crossed his arms over his chest.

"So, it sounds like you had a handful of her last night outside the dance." His dad waggled his brows. "If you know what I mean."

"No, actually, I don't." Grady did know. But he forced himself not to give his dad the reaction he was looking for.

"Everybody's talking about how you kissed her long and hard."

"Long and hard. Really, Dad?"

His dad's smile widened. "Okay, well, that's my interpretation after everything I've heard."

Grady should have known there would be gossip. After all, he'd hauled Clementine out of the dance over his shoulder, and even though he'd taken her away from the lodge, it had still been easy to spot them—or at least, Willa hadn't had any difficulty finding them.

Grady sighed. "It didn't mean anything. In fact, we were in the middle of a fight when it happened."

"Then it meant exactly what it was supposed to mean."

Grady bit back the question his dad was waiting for him to ask.

He didn't have to wait long before his dad kept going. "It means you care about her and she cares about you."

"If that's what you want to think, I won't stop you."

"It's not what I *think*; it's what I *know*." His dad

turned his attention back to the crate and retrieved a stack of scarves.

Grady forced himself to refrain from rolling his eyes.

Was all the gossip the reason why Clementine's admirer had followed her this morning? Maybe he'd heard the rumors and was upset.

His dad placed the scarves on the table next to the mittens and hats. "Guess that's one way to take the lead in our challenge. Does that mean if I kiss Mrs. Meriwether, I can regain my position?"

Grady didn't want to think about his dad kissing the middle-aged widow and feeling all the heat that came with kissing. "Can we stop talking about kissing?"

"I'm not the one who made the town news this morning with the kissing. That was you."

"It was a mistake, and it won't happen again."

His dad's grin was still firmly in place. "For a mistake, it sure sounds like you enjoyed it."

If he denied that he'd enjoyed it, his dad would see right through any excuses. Best thing to do was admit it and move on. "Of course I don't mind a kiss now and then. What man wouldn't?"

"But a kiss with the woman you're crazy about? That's something special."

"I'm not crazy about her."

"You can't tell me you're not counting the minutes until you can kiss her again."

"I'm not." Oh, he was. Which was why he'd hardly slept at all last night and why he was keeping well away from her today. Just the brief interaction in the livery and walking her across the street had overloaded his senses.

With mirth still lighting his face, his dad shook his head, clearly not believing him.

"Please. Let's focus on how we're going to keep Clementine safe."

"Sure." His dad settled a load of gloves on the worktable, then pushed the empty crate aside and gave Grady his full attention. "What else do you think we can do?"

Grady had been tossing around ideas during the long hours of his sleepless night. "She needs someone chaperoning her at all times until we catch the fellow who's harassing her."

He'd already gone over to the blacksmith's shop and given Jeremy Usher a good look at his fist. Of course, just like John, the fellow had denied having anything to do with spying on Clementine and leaving her notes.

"You know what I'm thinking?" Dad's voice was much too chipper, almost as if he was enjoying this whole affair.

Grady's runaway thoughts came to a halt. Dad wasn't behind everything, was he? In another attempt at playing matchmaker between him and Clementine?

Grady shook his head. No, his dad wouldn't stoop to

frightening Clementine, not even by making up the unnerving notes.

Dad sized up Grady. "I'm thinking there's one surefire way to make this all stop."

"Do I want to hear it?" Grady couldn't keep the sarcasm from his tone.

His dad chuckled. "Of course you do."

Grady waited, his arms still crossed.

Dad met his gaze head-on. "Best thing to do is marry her."

Grady snorted and pushed away from the worktable. "If you won't take this seriously, then I'll have to figure it out for myself." He aimed for the back door, frustration swelling in his chest.

"I *am* serious."

"No. You're not." Grady tossed open the door.

"Hold on now, son." Dad chased after him, his voice earnest.

Grady paused in the doorway but didn't turn around. He didn't have the time or patience for his dad's meddling.

"If you're not ready to marry her yet—"

"I'm not marrying her, Dad. Not now, and not anytime."

"At least pretend to want to marry her or get engaged," he rushed to explain. "If you do that, you might be able to draw out her stalker."

Grady stared unseeingly out the back door to the alley. Was it possible they could draw out the stalker? Maybe bait him?

Steeling his spine, he turned around, closed the door, and leaned back against it. "Okay, I'm listening."

Dad's shoulders seemed to relax.

Guilt pricked Grady. He was being too hard on his dad. After all, Dad cared about Clementine too. And he only had their best interests in mind.

Dad glanced toward the hallway that led back to the store, as if making sure they were alone. "The best way to flush out something undesirable is to put pressure on it."

"And pretending to get engaged will put pressure on the fellow?"

"Yes, since he made it clear he wants to marry her, he'll likely be upset at the prospect of losing her. And he'll come after you."

Grady nodded slowly. He'd much rather have the stalker engage with him than Clementine. He would be ready and would teach the fellow a lesson he wouldn't soon forget.

"You'd have an easier time figuring out who it is if you drew him away from Breckenridge."

"How would I do that?"

"Take Clementine someplace for a few days. Maybe to Georgetown. And see if the fellow follows you."

Grady's mind began to spin. That was actually a good

plan. They could stay in one of his dad's hotels. It would be better than sitting around waiting for more creepy notes and more spying. If the secret admirer was really serious about Clementine, he'd probably try to follow her. At the very least, it would give her a break from the harassment.

"I'll need a good excuse for leaving town with her."

His dad shrugged. "We'll tell everyone you're running off to get married. It's probably the only reason that will draw the stalker into following you."

Grady gave a firm shake of his head. "No. I'm not starting that rumor—"

"It's the best excuse, Grady. If word just happens to leak out that you and Clementine sneaked away to Georgetown to get married, he'll be on your trail soon enough to try to stop you."

"What if we tell everyone we're going to Georgetown because Clementine is interested in expanding her candy business there?"

Dad surveyed the pans on the table, their contents in one stage of the candy-making process or another.

Clementine had talked about expanding her business. What she really wanted was her own little shop that she could call Clementine's Confectionery. She'd told him that plenty of times back when they'd still been friends, and he knew her goal hadn't changed. But with the way she gave her candy away to the widows in town, all her friends, and even complete strangers, she'd never be able to amass enough of a profit to purchase her own place.

But that didn't matter at the moment. What they needed was an excuse for getting out of Breckenridge and traveling to Georgetown. One that preferably didn't involve pretending they were running off and getting married.

"I stick by what I said." His dad pinched off a piece of brittle candy and popped it into his mouth. "If you really want to catch her stalker, then you'll need to make him believe he's losing Clementine."

"But who's going to believe Clementine and I want to get married? With how much we fight, the stalker will realize it's not true."

"That's where you're wrong." Dad's grin made another appearance. "Everyone will believe it because they all see what I do—that the two of you give off enough sparks to light up the whole town."

Grady wanted to deny his dad, but last night there had been plenty of sparks. But even if the sparks were real and sizzling, they couldn't last, could they?

"Besides," his dad continued, "with the rumor of your kiss making the rounds today, it wouldn't be that far-fetched if you decided to run off to Georgetown, get married, and have a little honeymoon away from town."

Was his dad right? Maybe pretending to be engaged was the best option. "What will we tell everyone when we get back to Breckenridge? I don't want people assuming we're married."

"Tell them the truth. That you had to put up a ruse so you could track down the stalker."

"Good point." Grady let the idea settle inside.

It had been a month or more since he'd ridden to Georgetown to check on the businesses there. Over the past year, he'd been shouldering more of the supervision because his dad intended to one day hand the businesses over to him entirely. Their solicitor in Georgetown took care of most of the financial aspects, and his dad had put in place several excellent managers who oversaw the daily details of the hotels, restaurants, stores, and more.

Still Grady liked to visit and take stock of things too. He wouldn't mind getting in a trip before the snowfall made the forty-mile trek difficult. In good weather, he could make the ride in a day. Sometimes, if he got a late start, he stopped and stayed with a friend who lived in Summit Cove.

"The real question," Dad said with a challenging glint in his eyes, "is whether you can get Clementine to agree to the plan."

Grady pictured her upturned face from last night outside the lodge. He hadn't needed to try too hard to get her to go along with the kiss. If he could do that, surely he could persuade her to go along with the plan to keep her safe.

# 11

"Absolutely not." Clementine let her refusal ring out as she rolled the fondant around the chopped pieces of candied cherries and apricots along with the walnuts.

Grady blew out a noisy sigh. "Stop being so difficult." Standing in the middle of the kitchen with his ice skates draped over his shoulder and his knit cap covering his dark hair, he held his hockey stick in one hand and his gloves in the other.

It wasn't fair that he could go on with life as usual while relegating her to stay behind at the house for the evening. It was completely unfair. But after the stalking incident that morning and then the rose and note about marriage, she could admit she was reluctant to venture out.

Grady and Mr. Worth had both insisted she make her candy in the house kitchen for the evening instead of using the workspace at the back of the store. Although she didn't want to impose, she hadn't protested when Grady had helped her carry her supplies over for the chocolate-covered fruit she was making tonight.

Mr. Worth had asked her to play checkers with him once she was done, and she'd already eagerly agreed to the time with him. Even so, she was disappointed she couldn't go to the hockey game. She rarely missed one.

But the danger of her situation was becoming more of a reality, and she didn't want to be foolish and cause more trouble. Mr. Worth had indicated that if nothing else happened tonight, she could go to church in the morning with them. At least she had that to look forward to.

In the meantime, she had to be content with staying secluded at home. And she was finding that difficult, especially as she watched Grady preparing to leave for Mill Pond.

She couldn't complain about Mrs. Worth's kitchen, one that had been designed to accommodate candy-making and baking projects. The stove was massive, with two ovens—one on either side of the firebox. The walls were lined with countertops that allowed not only for additional workspace but also for plenty of area to cool and store all the goodies.

Mrs. Worth had adored her new kitchen, and Clementine had spent countless hours with her there, so working in the spacious room felt like being home. Even though she missed Mrs. Worth being there with her, she knew the dear woman was looking down from heaven and smiling.

Well, maybe not smiling over how much she and Grady were always fighting. Mrs. Worth had never liked it when they fought and had chastised Grady for it quite often during those last couple of years of her life.

"Leaving town is the best option." Grady's voice was testy, as usual.

"What if he doesn't follow us there?" She had all kinds of problems with the plan Grady had just outlined for taking her to Georgetown for a few days as a way to lure her stalker out of hiding and find out who he was.

"He might not. But . . ."

Something in his tone halted her production. "But?"

"If he finds out we're running off to get married, there's a good chance he'll follow and try to stop us."

She could only stare at Grady, speechless at his suggestion. Never in all her days had she expected a marriage proposal to come out of Grady's mouth.

At her lack of response, his expression took on an almost panicked look. "No. No. It's not like that at all."

So he wasn't actually proposing? Of course not. Why would he when he disliked her so much? But now that he'd started down that path, she intended to give him as much grief as she could. "I'm sorry to disappoint you, Grady, but just because we kissed last night doesn't mean I have any desire to marry you."

"I realize that." His eyes quickly narrowed.

"But of course"—she infused sugary sweetness into her tone—"if you have your mind set on it, I wouldn't want to break your heart and ruin your future plans."

He glared at her but didn't respond except to roll his eyes.

She bit back a smile. "I know how irresistible you find me—and now all the more so after how much you enjoyed kissing me."

"Don't flatter yourself."

"I'm not. I'm just stating a fact." She looked pointedly at his mouth, hoping to get another rise out of him.

He pressed his lips firmly together, but the tautness only stirred a strange heat inside her—a heat she'd felt last night when those hard lips had demanded she respond to his kiss.

Grady's jaw ticked, and he dropped his gaze to her mouth and lingered there, as if he was remembering exactly how the kiss had felt too. His eyes darkened, turning into charged storm clouds—clouds threatening to unleash on her.

Her teasing wasn't irritating him. Instead, he seemed to be enjoying having another charged moment together. He was probably gazing back at her mouth on purpose, taunting her in return.

Even though she didn't want to be the first to look

away, she shifted her attention to her sticky fingers.

No doubt he was gloating because he knew his looking at her mouth affected her more than hers had him.

"Then it's settled." He finished crossing to the back door. "We'll leave for Georgetown first thing in the morning."

"And pretend to be a happy couple running away to get married? No, thank you."

"We don't have to be happy. We just have to pretend to want each other." His voice turned into a low growl. "And you won't have to pretend too hard."

"Grady Worth!" With heat spilling into her cheeks, she flung a walnut at him. "I'm not pretending to want you—not when that's the furthest thing from the truth."

He tossed a smirk over his shoulder as he opened the door and stepped outside.

"I'm not going," she called after him. Spending a few days with him was a terrible idea. They could hardly get along for a couple of minutes, much less hours and hours. They'd end up killing each other.

He bent down and picked something up. When he turned back around, his expression was solemn, and he was holding another silk rose with another note.

Her heart fell, and she released the ball of candy, letting it drop back into the fondant mixture in the bowl.

Grady peered around outside, as if trying to spot the

culprit. Then, with a fresh scowl, he stepped back inside and closed the door. He didn't ask her permission to read the note but instead flipped up the sheet and scanned it.

When he was finished, he held it out to her.

As she took the rose and the slip, she tried to read his eyes and expression. But other than the gravity there, she couldn't determine anything more.

A part of her wanted to crumple up the note, toss it outside along with the flower, and echo Grady's shout from the other night to throw both into the toilet. But she suspected more shouting wouldn't do any good, especially because she'd told the fellow following her earlier today to stop with the notes.

With a quiver rippling through her, she forced herself to look at the print. *"I will kill Grady so that you can marry me."*

A gasp slipped from her lips. This man was more serious and dangerous than she'd realized if he was threatening to murder Grady. And he was obviously mentally unstable if he really believed she'd want to marry him after that kind of threat.

Grady remained silent by the door.

Her fingers tightened around the note and the rose, a new fear swelling inside. It was one thing for her to be in danger. It was another matter entirely to put Grady's life at risk. In fact, the very thought of him going out the door into the darkness sent a shiver down to her bones.

What if the fellow planned to attack Grady on his way to the pond? Or intended to shoot him? Even if not tonight, Grady wouldn't be safe anywhere he went. He'd always be in danger. Because of her.

The fear rose into her throat, and she had to swallow hard to force it down.

Grady was watching her and for once wasn't trying to irritate her.

She couldn't allow anything bad to happen to him, had to do whatever she could to put an end to the threat against him. If that meant she had to leave in the morning and pretend to run away with him to get married, then she'd do it. It would still involve some danger as they lured the fellow after them and tried to expose him. But in doing so, at least they would be taking some control instead of waiting for him to strike Grady.

She dropped the rose and note to the table. "Okay. I'll go."

He seemed to release a pent-up breath.

"But only if you stay home tonight."

He flipped open the door. "It's nice to know you're worried about me."

"I'm not." She was, but she didn't want him to realize how afraid she was for his life.

"Then I guess you're just eager to spend time with me." He took a step outside.

She started after him, determined to grab and stop

him if necessary. "You just got a death threat, Grady." By the time she reached the door, he was halfway across the yard.

"Admit it," he called back. "You want me all to yourself this evening."

"Grady Worth. You're impossible." He was so aggravating.

He lifted his hockey stick in a farewell wave, then he began to jog away.

She watched him for a moment longer until he turned the corner and was out of sight. She glanced around, half expecting her stalker to step out of the shadows and start toward her. With a chill racing over her skin, she rapidly closed the door and locked it.

She leaned back against it and pressed a hand to her thudding heart, praying Grady would be safe. As much as she wanted to deny that she cared about him, she wasn't fooling herself. Even though he was annoying, he was an integral part of her life and had been for years. And she didn't want to lose him.

12

Grady had a nagging urge to push the horses to go faster. He wasn't sure why, because he hadn't seen anyone on their trail for the past hours they'd been traveling.

Even so, he couldn't keep from looking over his shoulder every few minutes.

On a sturdy gelding ahead of him, Clementine rode with a proficiency he'd always admired. Of course, having grown up on a horse ranch, she knew horses better than most women, and she also knew how to guide a horse over mountain trails, which was helpful because he'd taken the route through Keystone that led to Argentine Pass. While parts were level and easy, other areas were treacherous, particularly those in the higher elevation that already had a snow covering.

Along the stretch of the Snake River they'd been traversing, the trail was relatively flat. It was filled with aspen trees that had already lost their leaves and the dark fir, spruce, and ponderosa pine trees that grew in thick stands all along the river valley and up the surrounding hillsides.

They hadn't come across many wild animals, had only spotted moose from a distance as well as a few deer. They also hadn't run into many other travelers.

He tipped up the brim of his Stetson and peered at the gray sky above them. Although the sun was hidden behind the clouds, he guessed it was midafternoon and they were due for another stop soon. They were making good time, and at the current pace, they would reach Georgetown at dusk.

They'd been careful not to be seen leaving Breckenridge that morning. The stalker likely wouldn't realize they were gone until Dad started the rumor that his son had run off with Clementine to get married in Georgetown. Even if the fellow rushed to follow them, Grady expected they would have at least a few hours' lead.

Regardless, he'd remained wary, and Clementine had kept a level head the whole time.

That was another thing he appreciated about her. She wasn't a frail woman who demanded coddling. Instead, she was independent and never complained. In fact, he suspected as long as she rode with him, she wouldn't let him know she needed to stop even if she were about to keel over.

The guilt that nagged him occasionally reared up,

because he knew he was at fault for the tension between them. He didn't want her to be unwilling to tell him when she was uncomfortable or needed a break. Maybe it was time to figure out a way to change that.

He peered ahead of her to the gradual uphill climb that led to the pass. They'd do well to stop before they reached higher ground. Once they started up Argentine Peak, they'd likely keep going until they descended the other side. He didn't like being on a peak in the afternoon with the way storms often blew in without any warning. And this time of year, the rain could easily turn to snow.

"Let's take a break at that bend in the river ahead," he called.

"I'm fine," she responded. "But if you need a break, then I'll give it to you."

He didn't answer, even though he was tempted to defend himself.

She urged her horse faster and moved well ahead of him.

She'd been talkative for most of the journey, and at times they'd had civil discussions about ordinary things like the people moving to Breckenridge, the new businesses being built, and even what was still needed in the high country.

He liked that he never had to come up with things to talk about with her. She carried the bulk of the conversation, and he could always speak his mind rather than saying what was expected.

He also liked that she didn't hang on to grudges for long. She'd been mad at him last night for leaving her to go play hockey—probably more worried than mad after the threat to his life. When he'd walked in the door later, she'd been in the middle of a game of checkers with his dad and had ignored him except for snippy retorts.

Later, he'd gone upstairs to find her already in bed, facing the wall with the lights out. He knew she wasn't asleep by how much she was tossing around, and he was tempted to apologize for his cavalier attitude toward his own safety. After all his nagging at her to be careful, it hadn't been fair of him to rush off. It probably seemed as though he had a double standard. The truth was, he hadn't done well in his game because he'd been thinking about her and all that was going on.

He'd planned on apologizing this morning once they were on their way, but she seemed to have put the incident in the past, chattering like she normally did. Since she'd apparently moved on from the issue, he'd decided to do so as well.

But maybe he needed to make more of an effort to iron out the tension. And he could start by apologizing for last night.

With a sigh, he nudged his horse to a trot to catch up with her. She was already dismounting by the time he reached her. As her skirt lifted, he got a glimpse of the trousers she wore underneath. The material clung to her legs, outlining the long length.

She'd also donned a thick great coat and battered black Stetson for the journey. But even with the rugged attire, she still had a womanly appeal that couldn't be hidden. The trouble was that she'd always been too pretty. And he hadn't wanted to be attracted to her but always had been anyway.

He slid down from his mount. As he started to stretch, he froze in place at the sight of her taking off her hat, bending her head, and shaking out her hair. The long waves had come loose and were wild and free and swirling in the breeze.

As she stood and flipped her hair back, his attention snagged on her neck and the taut line rising from her collarbone. She easily gathered her hair and began twisting it upward into a knot, but each move only emphasized the deftness of her fingers as well as her slender arms and shoulders.

"What's wrong?" She paused with her hair coiled, a pin sticking out from between her pursed lips. Her eyes were wide, the green light in contrast to the dark forest behind her.

A biting comment rose to the tip of his tongue—one about how she didn't have to try to look pretty for him out here. But he swallowed it. He had to start being more polite to her sometime. Why not now? "Was just thinking how pretty your hair is, that's all." It wasn't *all*. He'd been thinking about a lot more than her hair.

The truth was, he could understand why the stalker was infatuated with Clementine. She was the kind of woman a man could only dream about having.

At his compliment that didn't contain even a hint of the usual sarcasm, she remained in the same position, the pin between her lips and her eyes still wide. She clearly hadn't been expecting him to say something nice—because he never said anything nice to her anymore, and because he was a blasted cad pretty much all the time.

What had changed in his relationship with her to cause the rift?

The question was nagging him again today, just as it had the other night. Was it because they'd both moved from childhood into adulthood and he hadn't known how to handle her transformation into a gorgeous and desirable woman? Hadn't known how to handle the attraction he didn't want to feel toward a friend or the way his body reacted to her even when he didn't want it to?

Maybe in his confusion, he'd found it easier to distance himself, to pretend he didn't care, even to make himself dislike her in an effort to keep from thinking and dreaming about her.

Whatever the case, he didn't want to be that man

anymore. He had no reason to be that man. He understood now that he could be attracted to a woman physically and even find her beautiful. It was a normal reaction.

But he'd learned the key was what he did with his reactions—how he channeled his thoughts, how he resisted temptations, and how he kept from viewing women as objects for a man's pleasure.

He could do that with Clementine. He could acknowledge how stunning she was but also keep himself from getting carried away by selfish cravings that had no place in any relationship.

"I'm sorry for last night." He blurted the words before he could make any more excuses for not apologizing.

She still stood unmoving, one hand holding up her messy knot of hair and the other pressed against her chest. Her brows lifted a fraction, as though she was waiting for him to say more, to add a biting remark or to smirk.

"I shouldn't have run off the way I did." He kept his voice level. "It was hypocritical of me to expect you to hide away while I went out and made myself a target."

She dropped her hand from her hair, and it spilled in a glossy cascade all around her, making her even more stunning, especially as she gaped at him.

"Will you forgive me?" He needed forgiveness for a lot more than just his response last night, but it was a start.

She watched him another moment, narrowed her eyes, and then fisted her hands on her hips. "Of course I do. If you're serious about it. But since when are you serious about anything?"

He shrugged. "I'll try to do better."

Her mouth stalled around a ready response.

He ducked to hide his efforts to restrain a grin. He liked making her speechless. Maybe that needed to be his new tactic. It was better than irritating her.

Almost as if she was too flustered to fix her hair—or had forgotten—she slipped off the canteen she wore diagonally over her coat. She unscrewed the top, fumbling with it more than usual.

Oh yes. He liked this flustered Clementine a lot. He removed his canteen, easily popped off the cover, and took a large swig. Even if he knew he needed to be more polite with her, he was still a rogue at heart, and he wouldn't pretend to be someone he wasn't.

She tipped her canteen to her lips, but nothing came out. She glanced in the direction of the river, which was visible through a shadowed wooded area filled with boulders. "I'll fill my canteen and then we can get going."

He held out his hand. "Here. Let me."

She stared at his hand and then back up at his face.

Without giving her a chance to protest and be stubborn, he stalked over to her, took the canteen, and then strode away in the direction of the river. With each step he took, he could feel her gaze upon him, questions radiating from her.

He didn't turn around. But he was sorely tempted to stop and stare back at her, especially while her hair was down. He'd always loved seeing her with her hair unbound. In fact, the first time he'd met her, shortly after he'd moved to Breckenridge, he'd been practicing hockey with a broom and a ball in the alley behind the store on a hot summer day. She'd raced around a corner, soaking wet from having fallen into the river after failing a dare to walk across the railing of the bridge, and was trying to escape being seen by her ma, who was in town shopping.

At fourteen, he'd still been more interested in hockey than girls. And of course, she'd only been twelve, hardly more than a waif. But he'd loved her hair even then. He'd stopped his hockey game to help her get it untangled, and he'd even gone inside his mom's bedroom and found a brush and towel for her.

They'd become friends after that, and during the rest of the summer, she'd come to town several times a week to see him. If he was playing hockey, she'd chase after the ball for him. If he was doing chores, she'd help him. If he was going fishing, she'd tag along. Even back then, she'd done most of the talking, always having funny stories to share about her day or her family or the horses. She'd made him laugh and brightened his life when he hadn't known he'd needed it.

The truth was, those had been dark days for his family, especially the couple of years leading up to their move from Georgetown to Breckenridge. After years of miscarriages and struggling to conceive another child, his mom had gradually sunk into a heavy despair, on many days not even getting out of bed.

Grady hadn't understood at the time why his dad had initiated the move away from the town they'd lived in since Grady was three. But in hindsight, he understood that it'd had to do with his mom. His dad had wanted to take her away from the difficult memories weighing her down, and he'd hoped she could find a fresh start someplace new.

After the move, his mom hadn't adjusted right away. She'd still stayed in bed far too often, but she'd started making her candy again and had more energy than she'd had in a long time.

Then she'd met Clementine. Sweet Clementine had burst into her life like sunshine after a long, dark winter. Clementine had never met a person she didn't consider a friend, and that was how she'd treated his mom. Clementine had loved Mom with the same unreserved love she gave to everyone.

But a spring thaw was gentle, and the new blooms poked through in their own time. So it had been with his mom. The changes had been gradual, the return of life slow, and the joy had pushed through in small clusters.

Eventually, his mom had begun to spend more and more time with Clementine, especially as Clementine got older and became more interested in making candy. As a result, Clementine had stopped seeking him out as much. Maybe that had bothered him and affected his relationship with Clementine too. After all, Clementine had been his first friend in the new place—probably one of his best friends.

Whatever the case, Clementine had made his mom happy in a few short years, when he'd failed to bring her happiness during all their many years together.

The truth was, he'd never been enough for his mom. All those years when she'd been trying to have more children and failing, she'd never been satisfied with just him, had needed more than him in her life to be happy— or so it had seemed at the time.

Maybe he'd been jealous of Clementine's ability to win his mom's love. Maybe he'd even grown to resent her relationship with his mom. He wasn't sure. But he did remember one time after an argument with Clementine, when he was about eighteen. He'd stomped into the house to where his mom was working in the kitchen. She was standing in front of the stove, her face flushed and her eyes bright with tears.

"Grady, I hate when you fight with Clementine."

"She's so childish," he responded, having just admonished Clementine about her need to stop going barefoot because the fellows were making comments about her ankles and how pretty she was.

He'd demanded that she wear shoes around town. She'd hotly told him she'd do whatever suited her. Of course, he'd responded that the next time he saw her barefoot, he would tie her up and take her back to the ranch.

"Clementine is a good girl." His mom's beautiful face had already been growing thin at that point from the pneumonia that never seemed to go away. "You'll always take care of her and love her, won't you, Grady?"

He hated seeing her upset or in tears, so he agreed with her like he always did. "Of course I will."

"She's become the daughter I always wanted but never thought I'd have," his mom had said softly through a smile as a tear slipped down her cheek. She'd loved Clementine until the day she'd died, probably more than she'd loved him.

Grady released a tight exhale. He glanced behind him through the woodland to where Clementine was standing with the horses, still in the process of pinning up her hair.

Was it possible that, over time, he'd started resenting Clementine because he'd believed—rightly or not—that she'd stolen his mom's love and affection away from him?

A pinch in his gut told him that's what had happened and that things had only gotten worse when his mom had called Clementine a daughter. After that, he'd felt even more insignificant and unimportant to his mom.

With a heaviness filling his heart, he knelt among the small stones that lined the riverbank and began to fill Clementine's canteen. Yes, there were varied reasons why he'd pushed Clementine away as his friend. But he knew he'd finally landed on the biggest reason—he'd been resentful of her relationship with his mom.

But that resentment hadn't been fair to Clementine. It wasn't her fault his mom had never loved him the way he'd needed and hadn't been happy with just one child. And it wasn't Clementine's fault she was a vivacious and outgoing person who made friends easily.

He'd pushed Clementine away because of issues that had nothing to do with her and everything to do with himself and his own insecurities. Now, three years after his mom's death, he needed to come to terms with all that had happened with his mom and stop blaming Clementine.

At the crackle of brush near the riverbank beside him, he startled and glanced over to find a coyote crouched low to the ground and staring at him with dark, hungry eyes. It gave a low growl, revealing its sharp canine teeth.

Grady moved slowly, lowering his hand toward his revolver at his waist. He didn't think the coyote would actually attack him or that he'd have to shoot it, but he might need to scare it off.

Another growl came from behind him. Grady glanced

over his shoulder to find two more coyotes only an arm's length away. Before his fingers could close around his gun, the first coyote snarled and lunged, sinking its fangs into Grady's leg.

13

At a distressed shout from Grady, Clementine peered in the direction of the river, where he'd disappeared to a few moments ago.

Through the smattering of pines and craggy boulders, she glimpsed him along the riverbank, and he was swinging the canteens at an animal with thick brown fur, pointed ears, and long legs.

Her pulse spurted forward.

As Grady swung, another creature lunged at him from the other side, and then another.

There were three of them. Coyotes. And they were working together to attack Grady. He had his gun out, but with having to dodge all three at once, he obviously hadn't been able to take a shot.

She wanted to scream at him to run, but she was frozen in place and for a long second could only stare with growing horror.

As a canteen slammed into the head of one of the coyotes, it yipped and backed away. But in the same moment, another of the coyotes grabbed on to Grady's leg.

He released an angry roar and this time brought his gun down hard on the coyote's head so that it let go of him.

His roar penetrated deep inside Clementine, freeing her from her shock. With a pounding heart, she grabbed the rifle he'd stuffed into the holder behind her saddle. She aimed it toward the coyotes, but even though she knew how to shoot with some accuracy, she was too far away, and the coyotes were moving too fast. She also didn't want to risk hitting Grady.

She lowered the gun and glanced around for any other way to help him. Her gaze landed upon his horse, not far from hers. Could she scare the coyotes away by riding toward them with both of the horses?

She didn't know if that would work, but it was the only thing that came to mind.

Without wasting another second, she tucked the rifle under her arm and mounted. Before she was even situated all the way, she directed her horse toward Grady's and swiped up the lead line. Then, digging in her heels, she spurred her horse toward the woodland, Grady's horse trailing behind.

Even as she wound through the trees and boulders,

she urged her horse faster, thankful she'd learned to ride well as a young girl and knew how to stay in the saddle, even when she was holding a rifle and guiding another horse.

The pounding of the hooves and the trampling of the fallen leaves and pinecones drew the attention of two coyotes. They fell back as she rounded Grady so that the horses now acted as a barrier to protect him from the two.

Grady's hat had been knocked off, and he had a scratch on one cheek that was bleeding. But his mouth was set into a determined line.

"Get on," she called as she drew his horse around so that it stood between him and the lone coyote.

He glanced beyond her to the two coyotes who couldn't reach him without first going around her and her horse. His frown deepened, and he seemed about to say something, but then he swiped up his hat and the canteens, reached for his pommel, and swung up into his saddle.

"Let's go." She kicked her mount into action, heading back to the clearing the same way she'd come.

She could hear Grady right on her tail.

When they broke free of the woodland, she glanced back toward the river to see the coyotes standing tall and still watching them. She wanted to stop and make sure Grady was okay, but they also needed to put some distance between themselves and the hungry creatures.

She galloped onto the path and forged ahead. Grady followed close behind, and she guessed he wanted to get as far away as possible too. They rode hard for at least a mile or more before she slowed down.

The path was wide, so she let her horse fall into step beside Grady's. He'd put his hat back on, but he was cradling one arm, and the cut on his cheek was still bleeding. His denim was ripped on the lower half of his leg, and the dark material was wet with blood.

He'd been hurt worse than she'd realized. "We need to stop and take a look at your injuries." Although she'd packed lightly for her trip to Georgetown, she did have some basic toiletries in her bag strapped on to the horse. She had soap and a clean cloth for washing his injuries. And she could make bandages if necessary.

He peered over his shoulder, likely looking for the coyotes.

She didn't see them and doubted they'd follow so far. The breeze had also picked up, and a cold rain began to pelt them. It was all the more reason to stop. "Is there a shelter nearby?"

He pushed forward, picking up the pace again. "There's an abandoned mine shaft not far ahead and not too far off the trail."

"Are you worried about the stalker catching up to us?"

"I don't want to take a chance."

By now, most of Breckenridge—including the

stalker—was probably well aware that she and Grady had run off together. Hopefully they had a decent head start, and surely they'd be safe in an out-of-the-way hiding place while she doctored his wounds.

As they started the ascent, Grady took the lead. Eventually, he veered off the trail and into a gulch, continuing until he reached a rocky area, the sure sign that a mine had once been in operation with its leftover tailings and waste rock.

They had to search amidst the rock outcroppings and debris until they located an entrance. The cave-like mine opening had once allowed for mules pulling carts, so the two of them were able to bring the horses out of the cold rain even though it was cramped.

A narrow tunnel that led into the hillside was boarded up behind them. Shards of rocks and boards littered the floor, but a small area had been cleared for a campfire, where a few charred logs remained.

"Looks like someone else has stayed here." She began unstrapping her bag from the back of her horse.

"Some of the old-timers in the area know about the mine and use it as shelter at times like this." He nodded outside to the rain that was now falling heavily.

"It makes sense that you know of it, then." She lowered her bag to the ground. "Since you're so old, with one foot practically in the grave."

He lowered himself onto a slab of wood braced on

both ends by large stones and forming a bench of sorts. Though the cavern was shadowed and the stormy sky didn't provide much daylight, she could still see him wince.

He was obviously in pain—not only because he winced but also because he was sitting down. Grady wasn't the kind of fellow who could rest in the face of danger.

He reached for his pant leg that was ripped and bloody and began to tug it up, but with each inch, he went slower and his jaw clamped harder.

"Just wait, Grady." She unclasped her bag and dug through it. "I'll help you."

"I don't need help."

"Yes, sir. You do. Now sit still and let me take care of you."

Her fingers connected with the soap and clean cloth. Then she found her nightgown, which was light and could easily be ripped into strips to form bandages.

As she turned with the items, he was still working on his pant leg, and a soft groan slipped out.

Tsking, she knelt in front of him, then batted his hand away. "Grady Worth, you're as stubborn as an old goat."

"I know." His admission was soft.

She halted, her heartbeat sputtering just as it had a short while ago at the river when he'd asked for her forgiveness and said he'd try to do better. What was going on with him today?

He lifted his gaze and met hers. His dark eyes seemed even darker than normal, but they weren't filled with the usual anger or frustration at her. Instead, they held a gentleness that hadn't been there in a long time.

She wanted to ask him what was going on in that head of his.

But in the next instant, he closed his eyes, his face pinching with obvious pain.

For a few minutes, she tried lifting his trouser leg so she could reach his wound, but his calves were too muscular and the blood on his leg too slick.

"There's only one way to reach it." He kicked out of his boots, then pushed up from the makeshift bench and began to shed his coat.

As he did so, he revealed several other blood spots on his torso. One on his upper arm, where his shirt was soaked with blood, another at his side above his waist, and another on his backside.

"Oh, Grady." She couldn't keep the distress from her voice. "You're really hurt."

"Just a few scratches and bites is all." He dropped one suspender, then the other. And before she realized what he was doing, he let his trousers drop to the cave floor and kicked them aside so that he was standing in only his drawers, which exposed him from the knees down. At the same time, he began working at the buttons on his shirt.

Was he really undressing in front of her?

She took a rapid step back, a sudden flush moving into her cheeks. She wanted to tell him to stop, that he couldn't take off his clothes in front of her, that doing so was entirely inappropriate.

But she couldn't get her voice working. Instead, she stood there mutely as he finished unbuttoning his shirt and tossed it onto the heap of other clothing he'd already discarded. He wasn't wearing an undershirt, and his bare chest was right there in front of her. *He* was right there in front of her, nearly naked.

She was frozen in place, scandalized, unable to think of anything except that his body was perfection. His chest was rounded with muscles, his shoulders broad with sinews, and his arms thick with strength. Every inch of his skin was smooth, as if carved and polished out of the finest quality wood by a master craftsman.

In the process of calculating each of the cuts and bites on his torso and arms, he paused, as though realizing she was staring at him.

He straightened. "What's wrong?"

Ignoring the heat that was not only in her cheeks but also now seeping into her blood, she gave a pointed glare at the pile of his clothing. "This is indecent, Grady." She hissed the words, although she wasn't sure why, since they were the only two witnessing the indecency.

He glanced down at himself as if he hadn't realized he was indecent. Then he arched a brow at her. "I didn't think it would bother you since you've seen me like this plenty of times before when we went swimming together."

"That was different."

"How?"

"We were a lot younger." During those summer days after a hot afternoon of sitting in the sun fishing, he'd strip down to his drawers, and she'd take off her blouse and skirt, leaving on only her shift and petticoat. Then they'd splash around in the water and cool off for a while before drying out enough to put their clothing back on.

He shrugged. "There's not much about me that's changed between now and then."

She let her gaze dip to his chest again, then his arms. The heat flared hotter, spilling into her abdomen and setting her whole body ablaze. He'd always been good-looking, but he'd been somewhat gangly and skinny when she'd first met him, still in the phase between being a boy and a man.

But he was all man now. Totally and completely. And a swoony man at that. One she wouldn't mind staring at all day.

Except that he was injured, and this wasn't the time to salivate over his body as though she were some hussy. Besides, if he didn't think it was an issue to be unclothed

around her like this—so she could tend to his wounds—
then why was she making it an issue?

Maybe if she avoided looking at his torso, she
wouldn't think about how she wanted to run her hands
over his arms and shoulders and then down his chest so
she could feel each hard muscle.

"Done admiring me yet?" His voice was filled with
teasing.

"I'm not admiring you." She narrowed her eyes on
him. "I'm just assessing your wounds."

"Okay. Sure. Well, take your time *assessing* me."

She once again tore her attention from his chest and
dropped it to his leg. The bloody and torn flesh there
seemed to be the worst of the injuries.

Dragging in a breath of the musty, cold air, she
stepped back up to him. "Sit down and I'll start washing
the wounds." She pushed on those bare shoulders, letting
her hands linger there even though she didn't want them
to linger.

As he began to lower himself, a smirk curled up one
side of his lips, as if he was well aware that his unclad state
was ruffling her.

She stood above him and pressed her hands to her
hips. "You stop your gloating right now. I'm just
surprised, is all. And I'm sure you would be too if I tossed
off my clothes in front of you."

"Just admit, you like what you see."

She never would, not in a hundred years. "So I suppose you'd be okay with me shedding my dress?" She stood and shrugged out of her coat, letting it fall onto the growing heap of their clothing.

His cocky grin didn't waver.

She tossed off her hat and then began working on the buttons of her bodice.

He tracked her movements.

Was he really planning to let her unbutton her entire bodice? Of course, she had her chemise on underneath. But still . . .

As she neared the middle button, she let her fingers slow. The lacy edge of her chemise was now exposed along with some of her cleavage. She popped another button open and moved to the next.

She needed to stop. She was taking this too far. But now that she'd started, she couldn't show any weakness or hesitation.

She slipped open the next button, and her bodice slid off one shoulder.

With a strangled sound, Grady jumped up and grabbed both of her hands and tugged them away from her bodice.

For a long moment, he stood in front of her, her hands pinned in his, his body radiating tension, and his chest rising and falling rapidly. "Fine," he whispered, but the one word was strangely charged. "You made your point."

"What point?" She didn't want to stare at his bare body directly in front of her, but how could she not when he was so close and so beautiful?

"You're right. We're not kids anymore."

"So you don't want me to take off my clothing?"

"Do you want me to say what you want to hear?" His voice dropped low, so low that her stomach fell with it. "Or do you want me to tell you the truth?"

She was suddenly dizzy with a haze of wanting that seemed to rise up and grip her, tightening every muscle and nerve in her body. Whatever was happening between them was delicious, just like their kiss from the night of the dance.

But it was also dangerous. There had always been something about Grady that was slightly combustible, as if all it would take was a small spark to set them on fire and destroy them completely, along with the little bit of friendship they'd hung on to.

And she wasn't ready to let go of that little bit of friendship. As difficult as it had been to keep him from pushing her entirely away over the years, she'd held on this long, and she didn't want to do something they'd both regret, like kiss again. Or more.

She took a step back from him and swiftly began to rebutton her bodice.

Without a word, he grabbed his shirt from the top of the stack and stuffed his arms in. Then he lowered himself back to the bench, braced his elbows on his knees, and let his head fall into his hands.

"I'm sorry, Clementine." His whisper was so soft she hardly heard it above the patter of the rain outside and the breathing of the horses beside them.

She swiped up the soap and cloth. "I'm sorry too."

His shoulders were slumped. "No, it's my fault, not yours. I should have been more careful."

"It's all right." She unscrewed the lid of one of the canteens and poured water onto the cloth. "Now, let's get your wounds cleaned and bandaged."

It would be for the best if neither of them dwelt on what had just happened. In fact, it would be for the best if they forgot about it altogether.

14

The darkness outside the cave was thorough, not even broken by the stars or moon, which were hidden behind the clouds.

Grady added another board to the small fire he'd started to keep them warm in the dropping temperatures of the night. The rain had finally stopped, but not until after night had fallen. Although he'd traveled this route to Georgetown many times over the years, he didn't like to do it in the dark, and he'd made the decision to stay in the old mine until daybreak.

Clementine hadn't argued with him, had wanted him to rest after she'd cleaned and bandaged the worst of his bites. The one on his leg would need stitches where the coyote had ripped into his calf. Another bite on his upper arm had been deep. But the others were hardly more than scratches, and though they stung, they would heal soon enough on their own.

He didn't need to rest. He'd sustained worse injuries during hockey games over the years. But he'd let Clementine fuss over him anyway. And if he was honest with himself, he'd liked it.

Even now, as he added the slab, she frowned at him from her spot adjacent to him. "I said I'd take care of the wood."

"I didn't hurt my hand and can lift a piece of wood perfectly fine."

She glared at him, but it wasn't real anger, not tonight. And he liked that too, liked that she wasn't mad at him.

"You're a terrible patient," she said.

"I'm not a patient."

"Yes, you are."

He released an exasperated breath, except that he wasn't really exasperated.

She huddled beneath the blanket he'd insisted she wrap around her coat to ward off the cold air that snaked around them in spite of the fire.

He'd packed a bedroll, some food, and a few extra provisions in the saddlebags, as he always did whenever he made the long trip. The wilderness of the high country was sometimes harsh and unforgiving—as it had been today with the coyote attack—and he figured it was better to be prepared for emergencies.

They'd already split the canned codfish and canned

green beans he'd included. The fare hadn't filled him up, but it would tide him over. The horses had eaten too. After the rain had stopped, he and Clementine had led the horses out and let them graze in the tall grass nearby.

The saddles were now on the floor to lean against, and with the hour growing late, it would soon be time to try to get some shut-eye so they could leave as early as possible in the morning to stay ahead of the stalker.

He was hoping the rain had slowed the stalker and that he'd taken shelter someplace for the night. It was also possible the fellow had braved the rain and gone all the way to Georgetown.

Grady's greatest fear was that the man was close by and would spot their fire. But the old mine was far enough off the main trail that he doubted anyone would see the light—or at least, that's what he was counting on.

Either way, he wasn't subjecting Clementine to a night without heat. Even with the fire, she was struggling to stay warm, although she wasn't complaining.

"Your turn." Her green eyes were bright as she watched the flames dance.

"I don't know any more riddles." He leaned back against his saddle.

She'd kept them entertained for the past hours with her stories, antics, and games. "Then I guess I get another turn to tell one."

"You mean you get another turn to torment me."

"This one is really easy."

"They're all easy for me."

"That's because I only give you the easy ones."

"I solve them because I'm smart."

She snorted.

His lips quirked with the need to grin, but he held it back.

"There's a one-story house where the owner painted the walls green. He bought green sofas. His wife made green curtains to hang in the windows. And he even painted all of the doors green. So what color are the stairs?"

He rolled his eyes. "Really? That's a riddle?"

"Yes. Now answer it."

"It's too easy."

She smiled.

Every time she smiled at him tonight, it stole the breath from his lungs. He didn't want to stare at her and make another scene like earlier, when he'd taken off his clothing and then taunted her about taking off hers.

Just the thought of that moment made him want to pummel his head. What had he been thinking?

The problem was that he hadn't been thinking. And she'd made her point about how inappropriate it had been for him to undress in front of her. Oh, yes, she'd made her point very well—so well that he couldn't stop thinking about how sensual the moment had been, watching her undo each button, and how he could watch her do that every single night for the rest of his life.

A part of him couldn't believe he was actually considering what it would be like to spend his life with her. A day ago, he would have denied that he could have a future with her at all. But there was no sense in denying the desire that had been growing since the night of the kiss. Or maybe it had been there even longer than that. Had he desired her all these years but just been unwilling to admit it? Had he just been fooling himself with the talk of her being like a sister?

She'd plaited her hair earlier into a long braid that now hung over her shoulder, making her look carefree. "Okay, mister smart guy, let's hear your answer to the riddle."

"Do you promise that if I answer, you won't subject me to another riddle ever again?"

She pretended to swat at him. "No."

He watched her expectant expression, her lips parted just a little, her cheeks flushed. He knew the answer—there were no stairs because it was a one-story house. But he had the sudden need to see her smile again. "Of course the stairs were green—"

"Wrong!" She sat forward with a huge smile. "The house doesn't have stairs because it has only one level!"

Once again, his breath snagged at the beauty of her face. "What if there are stairs outside leading up to the house?"

"There aren't."

"Or stairs going down into the cellar?"

"The cellar has a ladder."

"Your riddle has obvious flaws."

"Not at all."

"In fact, I wouldn't even count it as a riddle."

She laughed softly.

The sound melted his heart, and this time he couldn't hold back a smile.

She was watching his face. "I like it when you smile."

"Of course you do." He hadn't smiled much around her—not when all they'd done was bicker. "Because smiling makes me look more handsome."

This time she did swat his arm. "No, I like it because it means you're not irritated with me."

Irritated? Was that what she'd assumed he'd felt toward her?

Grady stared at the fire. All the thoughts he'd had about his mom earlier in the day were still at the forefront of his mind, and he'd been mulling over his relationship with his mom and how difficult that had been. She'd always had a reticent nature and had tended to be less optimistic than his dad. Grady knew he took after her, and perhaps that'd had something to do with why he'd never felt as close to her as he had to Dad.

Whatever the case, he regretted that he hadn't been able to bridge the distance with her. But maybe it had never been his sole responsibility to close that gap. Maybe she should have done more to love him the way every child needed.

Thankfully, his dad had more than made up for his mom's neglect. Dad had shown him what it meant to be accepted for who he was. And he still did. He was a good father. Just one more reason to let go of the hurts that had lain dormant inside all these years.

Grady had to stop focusing on what he hadn't received and instead focus on all the good that had been a part of his life. And that good included Clementine. She'd been a bright spot in his life just as she had been for his mom.

He could feel her studying him, no doubt curious about the shift inside him. "I'm sorry I've been irritated at you."

Her eyes rounded. "Grady Worth, are you apologizing again? That's the third time today."

Leave it to Clementine to point out something like that. She never was afraid to talk about anything that needed to be addressed. "Don't get used to it."

"You're spoiling me today." Her voice held a note of teasing but also curiosity.

"I'm trying to understand myself," he started, wanting to give her an explanation without making excuses. "I've struggled with some feelings toward my mom—feelings of not being adequate enough for her."

Clementine gave him her full attention, her eyes radiating a warmth that beckoned him to continue. Even though she was a talker, she'd always been a good listener too.

"She always wanted more children, you know."

"Yes, I did know that."

"When she fell in love with you so easily, I think it made me wonder why she didn't love me as much."

"Oh, Grady." Clementine breathed his name tenderly. "She loved you more than anyone or anything after your dad."

He shrugged. "It's okay if she didn't. I'm coming to terms with it."

"But she did." Clementine sat up on her knees and reached for his hands.

He didn't resist as she wrapped both of her hands around his. Her fingers were cold, and he enfolded them in his to warm them.

"Every time I was with her, she talked about you all the time."

"She did?" His gaze connected with Clementine's. He wasn't sure why it was so important for him to see the truth in her eyes, but he searched for it there.

"You were her world, Grady. There's no doubt about that."

"I never felt that way."

Clementine pressed her lips together and seemed to

be formulating her next thought.

Even though the discussion was serious and important, her lips were distracting, especially when she pursed them.

"Do you think," she started slowly, "that when people are hurting inside, sometimes the hurt blocks the love from shining through? Sort of like clouds blocking the sunshine?"

Was that possible? Maybe his mom had loved him but had been so consumed with her own hurts and disappointments that it had clouded her love for him.

"Even though it might have been hard to see her love," Clementine continued, "please don't doubt that the love was there somewhere inside her."

He supposed if he looked back on his past, he had caught glimpses of her love from time to time. He didn't have all bad memories of his childhood. There had been good ones with her and Dad.

"Whatever the past"—he forced himself to stay where he was and not move closer to her—"I'm realizing that I have to let go of it. It's done and over. And I can't keep on making you pay for the problems I had with my mom."

"How are you 'making me pay'?"

"Blaming you and maybe even resenting how close she was to you and not me."

"So that's why you pushed me away?"

"I don't completely know. It could have been because we started growing up and weren't innocent kids anymore, and I didn't know how to handle all the changes."

She studied his face as if trying to make sense of what he was saying. He'd given her a roundabout answer to her simple statement about his spoiling her today with his apologies. But the apologies were past due.

"I don't know if I'll ever understand all the reasons I made you an enemy and not a friend, but it was all me, Clementine. Not you."

Her eyes rapidly filled with tears, and a small smile wobbled on her lips. "You're kind to say so. But I haven't always been nice to you either."

"Only because of me being a big oaf."

Her smile steadied. "Maybe that's partly true."

"Mostly true."

"Fine. I won't argue that you're a big oaf." She seemed to relax, her hands still intertwined with his. "Because you always have been an oaf, and that's something that will never change. And I don't want it to. I like that about you."

He let the tension ease from his shoulders. The simple truth was that Clementine had always accepted him for who he was, without holding anything back. And he'd missed her, missed that unconditional friendship, missed her companionship.

Was it possible he could rebuild what they'd once had? "I hope you'll forgive me and let me work at being your friend again."

She leaned into him, the tears welling in her eyes again. "Of course I forgive you, as long as you'll forgive me. And I want to work at being friends again too."

He nodded, his throat now tightening with the emotion of the moment. Before he could find the words to express his gratefulness to her, she slipped her arms around him and laid her head against his chest.

Was she hugging him?

He hesitated to wrap his arms around her in return. But as she melted into him, he couldn't help himself. He drew her into an embrace.

At the feel of her body against his, every nerve and every muscle was suddenly aware of her, but not in a friendship sort of way. No, his body was keenly attuned to her as a man to a woman—to the way she fit under his chin, the softness of her hair, her supple curves pressing into him, the firmness of her backside against his leg.

He tried to keep his mind from considering any of that. But she felt so good, and he wanted to bend in and nuzzle the stretch of her neck that he'd seen earlier when she'd unbuttoned her bodice and he'd gotten a glimpse of her chemise and the way it clung to her chest.

Swiftly he closed his eyes, as if that could somehow block out the memory. But he knew that no matter what he did or how hard he tried, he'd never forget that moment and would relive it often—even though he shouldn't.

"So, do you?" Her voice was soft against him.

Just the sound of it made him want to sink back and pull her down with him. "Do I what?" The question came out low and rumbly—more so than he'd expected.

"Forgive me?"

"Of course. Let's put it all in the past."

She released a sigh and squeezed him tighter. "Thank you, Grady."

He'd never held her so close before, and suddenly he had the overwhelming need to let his hands roam over her back and up to her shoulders and into her hair. He'd take out the braid, wind his fingers in deep, then angle her head back and kiss her all night.

The need was strong and urgent—and totally inappropriate since they'd just agreed to be friends again. A good friend wouldn't take advantage of his friend just because she was a beautiful woman and they were alone and stuck together for the night.

No, a good friend would put her interests above his own and take care of her, cherish her, and make sure she didn't feel he was using her or the situation in any way. Besides, just because he'd finally made peace with her didn't mean they would ever be more than friends. They may have kissed at the dance, but that didn't mean she was in love with him or would consider the possibility of love developing.

Did he even want her to consider the possibility?

A swift possessiveness rose inside him—one that said Clementine was his and always had been, and that's why he'd always gotten so angry whenever she was with any other man.

Along with the possessiveness was a burning for her deep in his soul. He couldn't remember not having had that feeling. It had been there from the first day he'd met her, and it had never gone away.

Was it love?

He swallowed hard, then dragged in a breath. He couldn't think about love. It was much too soon for that. After being at odds for so long, they needed time to be friends again and to have a normal relationship that wasn't so antagonistic.

Yet time wasn't something he had if he hoped to win the challenge with his dad. He had to find true love by Christmas, or he'd lose out on the loan for the building. Of course, his dad would gloat once he learned that Grady was finally admitting how attracted he was to Clementine. But attraction wouldn't win him the contest. His dad would expect him to make Clementine fall in love with him.

Maybe once they were through with this journey to Georgetown and had discovered who was stalking her, then he could see how their relationship was going. Even then, she was more important than winning the contest or getting a loan. And he'd never pressure her to have more than friendship just so he could beat his dad.

Yes, he had to focus on friendship for now. That was all. Especially tonight.

15

She was hugging Grady.

A part of her still couldn't believe it was really happening, but his solid body was flattened against hers and his arms surrounded her.

How had this happened? They'd started out the trip disliking each other, and now they were embracing like long-lost friends.

Her mind was still grappling with everything he'd just shared about his mom. She'd known Mrs. Worth had struggled with infertility after having Grady, but she hadn't realized how the issue had affected Grady. Maybe Mrs. Worth hadn't realized it either.

Clementine guessed that if Mrs. Worth had known, she would have tried to reassure Grady and show him better how much she loved him. Because she had loved him. She'd made that clear each and every time they'd made candy together in the kitchen.

A sweet relief was pulsing through Clementine—a relief that she and Grady no longer had to be at odds with each other. Even though he'd assured her that he was at fault for the distance, she couldn't keep from believing she'd somehow had a hand in it. A nagging in the far recesses of her mind warned her that she had to be careful not to push him away. She'd lost him once, and she didn't want that to happen again.

As much as she liked hugging him and feeling the closeness with him, she loosened her hold and began to sit up.

His arms remained tight, almost as though he didn't want to let go, but in the next instant, he released her and shifted back.

She scooted away too, dragging the blanket around her shoulders from where it had slipped down during the hug. The hard ground beneath her was cold, and the air in the cavern was chilled, even with the body heat from the horses as well as the warmth of the fire.

She couldn't keep from shivering and hugging her arms over her chest.

When Grady rose and began to rip several more boards from the tunnel entrance, she joined him, chastising him and bantering with him about which of them was stronger. They replenished the wood pile near the fire and settled back in.

As the flames flared, she moved in as close as she

could. Even so, only a section of her was touched by the heat, and the rest of her was still chilled. She tried to hold in her shudder, but it escaped anyway.

In the middle of her telling him a story she'd heard about a haunted mine near Breckenridge, he hefted up his saddle and then plopped it down directly next to hers. She halted her story midsentence and watched as he lowered himself beside her so that he was only inches away.

What was he doing?

He moved more slowly and stiffly than usual, probably because of his injuries.

"You need to be careful," she chastised, shifting away from him and trying to give him room.

He reached out a hand and stopped her. "Don't take this the wrong way, Clementine, but I've decided to sleep with you tonight."

She gasped.

A half grin worked at his lips, and his dark eyes seemed to taunt her. But the taunting wasn't malicious. Instead it was filled with something she didn't understand, something that sent a warmth pulsing through her.

His grin ticked higher. "With all of this handsomeness so near, I know it'll be impossible to keep your hands to yourself, but at least try."

She shook her head. "It won't be impossible for me.

But maybe you said that because you know it will be impossible for you to keep your hands off me."

At that, he reached for her and began to tug her closer.

"Grady Worth, don't you dare." She pushed at him, but her efforts to resist were only half-hearted. She trusted him completely and knew he'd never do anything unseemly.

He didn't relent. Instead, he rolled her and positioned her so that her back was pressed against his chest and in the crook of his body. Then he situated the blanket around her before drawing her closer.

With his arms and body cocooning hers, she settled into him, letting herself relax. Already, after just a few seconds, she was warmer than she'd been all night. And suddenly she knew why he was holding her—because he'd noticed she was cold and was coming to her rescue. He had no ulterior motives and wouldn't advance their relationship.

She didn't want him to advance it, did she?

Of course not. Having just forgiven each other for the hurts of the past few years, they were friends again. That was all.

Did that mean they could never become more?

She'd never thought of Grady as someone she might court, and she couldn't imagine flirting with him and fawning over him the same way she did other men. But she couldn't deny that an attraction had developed between them. She wasn't sure how, but after the incident with their clothing earlier, she'd been aware of his body in a way she never had before.

Even though she'd tried not to think about how he'd looked standing only inches from her, bare-chested, it was difficult to get the image of his muscled chest and thick arms out of her mind.

"Is this better?" His voice rumbled near her ear, sending more warmth through her.

She hadn't realized it, but he'd positioned her so that her front was facing the flames. He was heating her back and the fire her front. What more could she ask for?

"This is perfect, Grady." She relaxed into him even more. "Do you think this is okay?" Even though no one else was there to see them resting together in such an intimate fashion, she didn't want to do something wrong.

"You know you're safe with me, right?" Again his voice had a low, crackling quality—one that made her stomach tumble.

"I'm not worried about *you*." She situated her head on his biceps, loving the feel of him all around. "But what will people think of us staying together like this?"

"No one will know."

He was right. And she was worrying for nothing. Besides, they would already have all the gossip about their running off together to deal with when they returned. She wasn't sure how they would handle the rumors, but if Grady wasn't worried about the ramifications, she decided she didn't need to worry either.

"Finish telling me the ghost story," he said.

"Oh, I see how it is."

"How what is?"

"My story was scaring you, and you couldn't listen to any more of it until you knew you were safe with me by your side to protect you."

"That's exactly it." His tone held a hint of mirth.

"Very well. Then since I'm here to keep you safe, I'll continue."

They traded scary stories, and at some point she dozed, waking only when he moved away from her to add fuel to the fire. Each time he did so, she shivered until he wrapped her back up. And each time, she was cozy enough that she could almost imagine the two of them sleeping together at night forever.

It was a far-fetched thought, but it crept into her consciousness anyway.

She wasn't sure how much sleep Grady actually got, because whenever she awoke, he didn't seem to be sleeping. At daybreak, he gently woke her, then he rose and took the horses out. He let them graze, and by the time he returned, she had their bags packed and was ready to go. She wanted to clean his wounds again, but he claimed they were fine and that they would be at the doctor's office soon enough.

For the first hour or so, they were able to ride at a decent pace even though they had only faint light to guide their way. By the time they started on the switchbacks to Argentine Peak, the sun was out and the clouds of the previous day were gone. And thankfully, they didn't come across any ice or snow until they crested the top. Though a fresh layer covered the summit, it was only a few inches deep, not enough to prevent them from crossing.

They had to make their way slowly and carefully for a while, but by the time they started down the other side, the way was clear again. When they arrived at the old wagon road, they stopped to rest and water the horses. The rest of the way was easy terrain, and they made up for lost time.

As they reached the outskirts of Georgetown, they passed by a large mine that was busy with men at work. Grady slowed and seemed to take stock of everything. After the way he'd pushed them hard all morning, she raised her brow at him. "I didn't know you were interested in mining."

"My dad has part ownership of this mine."

"He does?"

Grady had narrowed his gaze on a fellow standing at the side of a tall tower that had pulleys. "He and his partner filed the claim when they moved to Colorado back in '60."

"So your dad was part of the early gold rush?"

He nodded.

"And the mine is producing all these years later?"

"It's still going strong."

"With gold?"

"And some silver."

She scanned the area, this time with a fresh interest. With multiple log buildings and smoke pouring from the chimneys of each one, the mine was like others she'd been at over the years, perhaps larger and more organized.

"When you said you needed to check on your dad's business in Georgetown, I assumed it was another store."

"Yes, that too. Along with a few other places."

They'd slowed almost to a stop, and she could only stare at Grady and try to understand the information she'd just learned about him and his family. His dad was part owner of a successful gold and silver mine and had been for close to twenty years. He had to be a wealthy man. Probably very wealthy.

She frowned at him. "Why didn't you tell me?"

"Tell you what?"

"That your family is rich."

He returned the frown. "Because it doesn't matter."

"It matters to me."

"Why?"

"I don't know. Because maybe it makes me feel like I

don't know you as well as I thought."

"It's not my wealth. It's my dad's."

"Even so . . ."

"I bought the livery with my own hard-earned money." He nudged his horse forward, and she stared at his broad back and stiff spine.

The road had widened and was covered with gravel. In the distance, above the evergreens, several streaks of smoke rose into the blue sky. They were getting closer to town. And possibly the stalker.

She caught up and rode alongside Grady, tossing him a sideways look. The day-old scruff on his jaw was dark. With his hat pulled low, his eyes were more shadowed and darker than usual. "So you've never taken any money from your dad?"

He clamped his mouth closed and stared straight ahead.

"You have." She wasn't sure why it mattered, except that maybe she was hurt that he hadn't trusted her enough to share this part of his life with her before.

"No, I told you, I bought the livery on my own."

Something in his tone told her there was more. "But . . ."

He rode silently for several heartbeats before expelling an exaggerated sigh. "But my dad has offered me a loan so I can buy the building next to the store."

She'd known the drug store was moving locations just

as soon as the new building was finished. When she'd first heard the news, she'd had the fleeting wish that maybe she could open her own candy shop there—the one she'd always dreamed about having. But she would never be able to purchase the building, not with the meager earnings she made. And she wasn't sure she'd even be able to afford to rent a space either.

"What do you want to do with the building?"

"Start a hardware store."

A hardware store. Grady had a good business mind and had no doubt already investigated the need for a hardware store and also calculated the costs, risks, and all the other business terms he tossed around from time to time.

"Your dad isn't giving you the money?"

"I'd never take a handout, and he knows it."

She'd always admired Grady for how hard-working and determined he was. And her esteem only grew at the realization that he could have used his father's success to further his own, but instead he was doing things on his own.

Grady sighed. "It feels like I'm cheating to even consider taking his loan."

Her mind filled with the image of the two-story structure next to the general store. It was weathered and needed a fresh coat of paint, and it was a little smaller and narrower than the store. But it was well-built and sturdy and clean. It would be a good spot for a hardware store, on Main Street next to the general store, and it would draw a lot of attention and customers.

"It's not cheating," she said. "You'll pay him back eventually."

"It wouldn't take me long, since I've already saved plenty."

"Then I don't understand the problem."

His jaw ticked, highlighting the raw, red coyote scratch on his cheek. "Remember when I told you my dad thought it was time for him and me to find wives?"

How could she forget? "Yes, and I also remember how you failed with Willa, candidate number one."

"She wasn't right for me."

"Really?" Clementine couldn't keep a tiny amount of glee from forming inside. "Willa's such a sweet girl."

"I think I know what I like in a woman and what I don't." Grady's voice turned testy.

"Fine." She wanted to pester him to tell her his ideal woman, but the words stuck in her throat. What if he listed off qualities she didn't have? Not that she cared if she had what he was looking for in a woman. Did she?

"Anyway," Grady continued. "My dad proposed a challenge."

She had an idea of what the challenge entailed, and she didn't have a good feeling about it.

"If I find a woman first, then he'll give me the loan."

The upcoming dinner with Mrs. Meriwether was suddenly making much more sense. "What happens if he finds a woman first?"

Grady shifted in his saddle but didn't respond.

It had to be something Grady didn't like. "Tell me."

"It's frustrating, that's what."

"What?"

He shook his head. "He said he'll pick a woman for me."

Everything within Clementine halted. In fact, she almost halted the horse. "Don't you think that's taking the challenge a little too far?"

"Absolutely."

"So you turned him down."

"Not exactly."

"Grady Worth." This time she did halt. "You can't let your dad pick a woman for you. This isn't the Middle Ages."

He reined in his horse too. "I wasn't planning on losing and letting him pick."

"You've already lost Willa. And you don't have many more options left."

He shrugged with an irritating arrogance. "I'll find someone."

Which was the worst option? Having Grady hastily find a wife or having his dad pick a woman for him? Neither sounded great. But she couldn't fault Grady for wanting to take up his dad's challenge. If it had been offered to her, she would have accepted it too.

"Who else do you have in mind?" Clementine mentally flipped through the eligible women in Breckenridge. She couldn't recommend Captain Moore's daughters—not after the way Sadie had hurt Ryder. There was Scarlet Noble, but at eighteen, she was too young for Grady, wasn't she? Of course, Violet Berkley and her sister had just returned to the high country after being gone most of the year out East with their mother. But who would want Violet after she'd run away from Sterling Noble right before their wedding last spring?

A few other possibilities sifted through Clementine's mind, but no women that she could see partnered with Grady.

"Well?" she persisted. "Who do you want to marry?"

16

Grady hadn't meant to tell Clementine about the challenge with his dad, but now that it was out, he was relieved.

"Do I need to pick a wife today?" he asked as he shifted in his saddle.

The wagon path was muddy with yesterday's rain. The long grass on either side was yellow and wilted and damp. But the way was level and smooth with wide open fields for most of the rest of the way to Georgetown, which was a good thing, since the coyote bites were hurting more than he wanted to admit.

"This is serious, Grady." She gave him a severe look. "You're a good man and deserve to be happy with the right woman."

His lips quirked up with another grin. He liked that she wanted him to find the right person, and he liked that she was taking the matter seriously. It meant she cared about his future and about him.

"But since you're grinning, clearly you're cavalier about the whole matter." Her tone came out laced with a frustration he hadn't expected.

He slid her a sideways glance, his brow rising. "What? Do you want me to give you the name of another woman I'm interested in?"

"Yes."

"Too bad. I'm not doing it." Not when that woman was her.

As soon as the thought filtered through his head, he clutched at his reins tighter, a sudden premonition radiating through him that the conversation was about to take a turn in a direction he wasn't sure he wanted to go yet.

He couldn't tell her he was possibly in love with her and had been forever. And he couldn't tell her he wanted a future with only her and was willing to wait, even sacrifice the hardware store, so that he could find a way to build a relationship with her.

Her green eyes had begun to flash now with her feisty anger. "You don't have a name. That's why you refuse to give me one."

"It's private."

"It's nonexistent."

"Think what you want."

She huffed out an irritated noise. "Who do you think

your dad will pick for you, since he's obviously going to win?"

Should he tell her the truth? The fact was, if his dad fell in love with Mrs. Meriwether and won the contest, then no doubt he'd make a big deal about matching him with Clementine. She'd find out soon enough anyway that she was his dad's choice.

"He must have someone in mind," she persisted.

Grady hesitated.

"Tell me."

"You're a pest. You know that, don't you?"

"Gra-dy."

"Fine." He released a breath. "You."

She fell silent.

When he slid another look her way, she was peering ahead down the wagon path.

What was she thinking? Without seeing into her eyes, he was having a hard time gauging her reaction.

"He loves you as much as my mom did. You know that."

She nodded.

That reason wasn't the whole truth. But how could he explain that his dad had also seen past the walls of defense and fighting to the love Grady carried in his heart for Clementine?

After holding her for most of the night, he knew without a doubt that he'd never love another woman the way he loved her. With her sleeping against him so peacefully, for the first time in a long while he'd felt at peace too. And he'd felt complete, as if he'd found a piece of his life that had been missing.

She nudged her horse forward again, and he followed suit.

"Will you say something?" he asked after a minute of silence. "Anytime you're silent, I get nervous."

She tossed him a wry smile. "Funny."

"No, really. Tell me what you're thinking."

"Your dad's sweet to want me to be with you, and I love him too."

"But you won't let him play matchmaker between us?"

She was silent another beat—a beat that seemed to last an eternity. Finally, she spoke, her voice quiet. "As nice as your dad is, I don't know that I could have an arranged marriage. I was hoping to marry someone I love and who loves me in return."

Someone I love. A knot cinched tight in his gut at the prospect of her loving any other man. "Who's that?"

"I don't know yet."

"Yet?" His voice turned hard, but he couldn't help it. "Then you have someone in mind?"

"I didn't say that."

"But you do?"

"What?" She gave him an ingratiating smile. "Do you

want me to give you the name of the man I'm interested in?"

"Yes."

"Too bad. I'm not doing it."

At the echo of his own words coming from her lips, he just shook his head. He couldn't expect her to share when he hadn't. Even so, frustration pulsed inside him, just as it always did whenever she was around other men. The fact was, he loathed anyone who might be able to win her affection. Somehow, he had to figure out a way to direct it toward himself.

In the meantime, he didn't want her to feel any pressure as a result of his dad's challenge, especially not after they'd just begun to tear down the barriers. He didn't want to put any more up. "Don't worry about my dad and his matchmaking. I'm not letting him push me into a relationship. I'd rather lose out on the building first."

"But it's an ideal location for a business."

He shrugged. "I'll save up enough on my own, and eventually I'll find something else."

"So if he told you to marry me or lose out on the loan, you'd rather lose out on the loan?" Something in her voice seemed to hint at hurt.

Was he projecting that he didn't want her? If so, that wasn't true. But how could he suggest he was open to a future with her but not scare her away?

"I see how it is." Her tone dropped low. "I'm good enough to be your friend, but I'd never be good enough to be your wife."

"No!" The retort came out swiftly. "That's not it at all."

"You find the thought of marrying me so repulsive that you'd rather turn down a loan than even consider it."

He reined in his horse, even though he was in a hurry to get to town, where they would be safer from the stalker than out in the open. But her assumption was so not true—the opposite of true—that he had to say something to clarify the matter.

She halted too and shifted in her saddle so that she was glaring at him.

"Of course the thought of marrying you isn't repulsive." It was not only *not* repulsive; it was a very, very enticing possibility. "And you're most definitely good enough for me. In fact, you're too good for me."

The frown lines in her forehead softened.

"I won't deny that I've felt some attraction to you." That was an understatement. He'd felt a lot more than *some*. "How could I not? You're an amazing woman."

"Amazing?" Her ire was completely gone now, and her lips curled up with a happy smile.

"And you're beautiful."

"Do you think so?" Her question was filled with such innocence that he knew she wasn't fishing for a compliment. Instead, she was genuinely surprised at his praise.

He was a worse cad than he'd realized for making her doubt how amazing and beautiful she was over the years. "You're incredible, and I'm sorry if I made you feel otherwise over the years. The truth is, I can't think of any other woman I'd want more than you."

As soon as the words were out, embarrassed heat swelled up, and he couldn't look at her. He didn't want to see her reaction to his almost-proclamation of love. Had he been too rash in stating his feelings so clearly?

"Thank you, Grady." Her response was soft, almost as if she was embarrassed too.

He hadn't meant to make things awkward between them, but that's what he got for being too open. "I just don't want to use you to get a loan from my dad. That's all."

"I understand now. And I respect you for that. I really do."

They started forward again and rode in silence for several long minutes, and he wished she'd start talking again about something else.

"So . . ." Her voice held a note of mischief. "You really think I'm amazing and beautiful?"

He rolled his eyes at her, relieved she wasn't taking everything too seriously. "Don't let it go to your head."

"Oh, I'm taking the compliments very seriously. In

fact, I'd like you to write them down so I can use them against you next time you get upset at me for flirting too much."

Flirting? His mood darkened, as if a cloud had swept in and covered the sun. "You do realize I'm the only one you can flirt with now?" His tone was dark and ominous too.

She quirked a brow at him.

"While we're in Georgetown." He wanted to demand that she never flirt with anyone else ever again, but he'd already said too much.

"So, you're giving me permission to flirt with you?"

"We have to put on a convincing show that we're in love and ready to get married."

"I can be convincing." She tossed him her classic flirtatious smile, the one that was half-cocked and followed by a wink.

"That smile is too fake." He didn't like it—never had. Probably because it had been directed at other men and not him.

"Okay, how about this?" She lowered her lashes and gave him a sultry look.

"No." He didn't like that one either for the same reason.

For several minutes, she practiced her repertoire of flirtatious moves on him. And he only got more irritated with each one.

"Don't do any of that," he groused as the edge of town came into view ahead.

Her expression lost the flirtatious pout and returned to normal. "You don't like any of them?"

"None."

"No wonder you don't have a woman yet," she snipped back. "You're impossible to flirt with."

"Come up with something new for me."

"New?"

"I've seen you use all those moves with other fellows, and I don't like them."

"My, my. Are we picky or what?"

"I could do better than you."

"I doubt it very much. I don't think you'd know what flirting was if it walked up to you and smacked you in the face."

She was right to a degree. He wasn't a charmer. He was much too straightforward to play games with a woman. But today he'd have a little fun trying to win her over without her realizing that's what he was doing.

"I'll teach you how real flirting is done," he said.

Her smile kicked up. "I'll look forward to it."

He intended to make sure she would look forward to it . . . today and always.

17

Clementine wanted to fan her hot face, but she was trying hard to act normal.

Grady was good at flirting. Really good.

He held her hand at the center of the dining room table and rubbed his thumb slowly across her knuckles.

Every time he did, her stomach quivered like violin strings being played by a bow, so that her body was now tight with a need she didn't understand.

The dining room of Brighton Hotel was busier than she'd expected. With its fancy wallpaper, several chandeliers, and elegant tableware, it clearly attracted finer guests than the usual simple dining rooms that catered to miners and other laborers.

Though she and Grady had a more private table near the back of the room, everyone seemed to be watching them, just as they had been all day everywhere they'd gone.

From the moment they'd ridden into town, they'd been the center of attention, especially because it seemed as though everyone knew Grady Worth—probably because the Worths owned half the town, from what she'd gathered.

In addition to Grady's popularity, people were observing his interactions with her out of curiosity. Everywhere they went, he let people know she was his fiancée and that they were in town to get married.

No doubt they were also watching Grady's flirting. How could they not, when he was constantly doing something?

At the livery, when he'd helped her dismount, he'd made a point of lowering her so that her body had briefly touched his.

When they'd walked down the street to the doctor's office, he'd held her hand, and he hadn't let go during the suturing of his wounds.

He'd put his arm around her when they'd checked into Brighton Hotel. The manager, Mr. Curley, knew Grady because the hotel was one that belonged to the Worths. Grady had introduced her as his soon-to-be wife and had asked for two rooms.

When Mr. Curley had teased him about only needing one room soon enough, Grady had given her a half-lidded look that had smoldered and made her flush. And it still made her flush whenever she thought about it. Although he'd only been pretending, something about it had been intense and had made her think back to when he'd undressed in front of her the previous day.

For the rest of the afternoon, Grady had given her a tour of Georgetown, showing her some of the other businesses his family owned, leading her past his childhood home, and introducing her to friends, managers, and too many other people to keep track of.

All the while, he'd touched her tenderly, sometimes at the small of her back, sometimes on her arm, and once even her cheek. He hardly ever smiled, and today had been no exception, but as he'd flirted with her, his gaze had kept seeking hers out, communicating silent messages like how beautiful she was and how proud he was to introduce her to people and watch their reactions when he called her his fiancée.

Every touch and every gaze had gone deep, unraveling her insides until she was strangely undone yet ready for him to do more—although she wasn't sure what that *more* entailed.

Now, as they finished their supper, she could admit he'd won the flirting challenge. He'd flirted so well all day that she was half tempted to round the table, plop down on his lap, and kiss him.

As if hearing her thoughts, his gaze dropped to her lips. Something flared in his eyes—something so hot that it sparked a blaze in her stomach.

The heat pulsed to her cheeks again, and this time she did tugged her hand from his and fanned her face. "Grady," she chastised softly. "You have to stop."

"Stop what?" His voice held false innocence.

"Everything."

"There's nothing wrong with holding my fiancée's hand." He reached out and captured her hand again. This time, he lifted it to his lips and brushed a kiss against her knuckles.

At the featherlight caress, she couldn't hold back a shudder of pleasure. His mouth was touching her, and that stirred her more deeply than anything else.

As he lowered her hand back to the table, a small smirk lifted the corner of his mouth.

"You're terrible."

He shook his head, his smirk widening. "No, I'm good at this."

"You're better than I expected."

His full smile blossomed.

Oh, heaven have mercy on her poor soul. His smile easily slayed her and turned her breathing shallow. She'd always loved his smile, and she couldn't resist reaching across the table now and touching his lips and that little scar below his mouth.

Her move was way too bold. She realized that the moment her fingers connected with his mouth and his smile faded.

"I'm sorry." She started to pull away, but he captured her hand and held it against his lips. Then, as his dark gaze hypnotized her, he pressed another kiss to her fingers. It wasn't soft and sweet like the other one. This one was hard and hungry and stirred hunger inside her.

What was happening to her? To them?

He didn't immediately drop her fingers, as though he sensed her question and wanted to answer. But at a crash across the room, she startled and hopped back, jerking her fingers free.

His attention swung to the dishes on the floor, then to the retreating form of a man hurrying out the door. Grady was on his feet in an instant, his expression hard, his eyes upon the man.

In a long great cloak with the collar pulled up and a derby hat pulled low, the stout form of the man was familiar. Was he the same fellow who'd stalked her back in Breckenridge?

All day, they'd been looking for signs of the stalker lurking nearby, but they hadn't spotted anyone unusual. In fact, over dinner, she'd finally relaxed, deciding that their plan hadn't worked after all, that the stalker hadn't followed them to Georgetown.

Grady hadn't agreed with her. He'd told her it was still possible the fellow would show up—if not today, then tomorrow. And he'd been right.

Without a word to her, Grady bolted away from the

table. With his nimble hockey-playing skills, he dodged several tables as he made his way to the door. The stalker was already outside, and the door closed firmly behind him. But Grady wasn't far behind and exited a moment later.

Amidst the curious glances from the other diners, Clementine started across the dining room after him. At the coat tree beside the door, she grabbed their coats and hats, but she didn't stop to put on her coat, unwilling to be left behind. She stepped out of the establishment and into the darkness of the November evening. Even though the windows of the hotel were lit, the boardwalks were shadowed, as were the narrow passageways between the buildings.

She walked down a short way to where Grady was standing in the middle of the street, pivoting and scanning every person passing by or lingering outside other buildings. But there was no sign of her stalker anywhere.

It was almost as if he'd vanished into the air. Where had he gone so quickly?

With a carriage rattling down the street toward him, Grady stepped out of the way and then crossed the street back to her, all the while continuing to scan the area.

As he reached her, he halted and dropped his hand to the small of her back. "Did you see him?"

"Not even a hair." She knew Grady didn't mean

anything by his touch, but the barest skim of his fingers sent a shimmer of pleasure through her. Not only did she like the pressure of his hand, but she also liked the possessive feel of it, as if he was making a claim on her.

It was just pretend, wasn't it? Then why did it feel so real, like he was telling the world she belonged to him?

A cold gust blew against her, but she didn't have time to shiver before he was wrapping her coat around her. Within seconds, he had her tucked into the crook of his body and was guiding her back into their hotel. Soon they were in her room and quietly discussing the stalker.

Even though she knew it was inappropriate for Grady to be seen coming and going from her hotel room, she didn't want him to leave her alone. She was embarrassed to tell him she was afraid, so she invited him to pull in his chair and play a game of cards with her.

With the night table between them, they played cards until she couldn't hold back her yawns. After he dismissed himself, she readied herself for bed and climbed under the covers. She curled up and tried not to think about the fact that their plan had worked and her stalker had followed her to Georgetown.

With him here, how would it all end? She suspected that the next time the stalker came around, Grady would chase him down again. But then what? If Grady caught the fellow, what would he do to him? Take him to the sheriff and ask for him to be put in jail? They had the roses and notes to use as evidence against the fellow, but would that be enough?

On the other hand, what if Grady followed the fellow and got hurt? They didn't know who this man was or what he was capable of doing.

Either way, luring the stalker to Georgetown was dangerous, and anything could happen.

At the rattle of her door, she sat up quickly in bed, her heart thudding. Was Grady coming back? Or maybe her stalker had figured out where she was staying and was breaking in.

A key twisted in the lock, and she clutched the covers around herself, as if that could somehow protect her if it were the stalker.

As the door opened and someone stepped inside, she swiped up her pillow. Without any lighting to distinguish who it was, she threw the pillow in the general direction of the door, hoping to at least startle the person.

"It's just me, Clementine," Grady whispered.

"You should have warned me you were coming in."

"I didn't want to disturb you if you were already asleep."

"Oh." She flopped back onto the remaining pillow. She heard him latch the door and turn the lock. A moment later, a pillow landed back on the bed, on top of her.

"Next time, throw a shoe or something hard." His

tone was wry. "That might actually hurt someone."

"I was in a hurry and threw the first thing I could find."

"Obviously."

He was crossing toward the bed, and his presence only served to remind her of the previous night in the mine cavern, when she'd slept against his chest. She was tempted to suggest that he lie down beside her and they have the same sleeping arrangement tonight.

But she knew they couldn't. They were in a public place, and people would talk about them. They had probably already caused gossip with Grady's presence in her room earlier. Besides, she didn't need the warmth from him tonight. The room had a small coal stove that was putting out sufficient heat.

He pulled out a chair beside the bed, positioned it so that he could see the door and her bed, then sat down. Even though she couldn't see his expression in the darkness, she could see his outline and the rigidness of his shoulders.

"What are you doing?" she whispered.

"I couldn't get enough of you today, so I decided to sit beside you all night." If not for the slight note of sarcasm in his tone, she might have believed him. She wished he really did want more of her. But she guessed he'd come to keep watch over her now that they knew the stalker was in town.

She relaxed into her pillow and tugged the covers around herself. She needed to tell him to go back to his room and get some sleep, especially after last night, but she truly didn't want to be alone.

How many days and nights would they have to pretend they were getting married before they caught the stalker? What if he kept evading them, just as he had in Breckenridge?

"How are we going to catch him, Grady?" she whispered. "We can't stay here indefinitely."

He sighed wearily. "We'll need to go to the church tomorrow morning and pretend we're getting married."

She sat straight up and shifted to face him. It was one thing to pretend to be his fiancée today, but it was another thing entirely to go to a church and perpetuate a fake marriage. "I won't do that, Grady. Marriage is sacred, and I don't want to go through the motions of a ceremony unless I'm truly getting married."

"We probably won't even need to start the ceremony before he barges in and tries to stop it."

Just the prospect of that happening made her shiver. "There has to be a better plan."

"I've been thinking about it since we left the restaurant, and a wedding ceremony is the only way we can trap him."

"Not only is it sacrilegious, but it's too dangerous."

"I'll line up the sheriff and some others and have

them hide around the church, ready to grab the stalker when he comes in."

"Maybe he'll be expecting that."

"Or he might be so desperate to stop you from marrying me that he'll do anything to get you."

She hated to think of what could go wrong, of someone—Grady—getting hurt, especially because of the last threat from the stalker about killing Grady. But what else could they do?

If only she'd been more careful with her interactions with fellows all along. After today and all of Grady's flirting, she could understand just how easy it was to fall for someone who was doling out attention and flattery, because she'd fallen for Grady. As tender and sweet as he'd been, he'd won her over in no time.

The truth was, he'd won her over a long time ago. And now, his confessions and apologies seemed to be giving her permission to acknowledge all the feelings for him that had already been there from the years they'd been friends. Not only had he been one of her best friends, but she'd also been on the verge of falling in love with him when he'd rejected her, which was probably why she'd been so hurt and angry when he'd pushed her away.

And if he had issues with his mother, was it possible that maybe she also had issues with her past that she'd ignored? Issues that had influenced how she'd related to

Grady? After all, he wasn't the only one who'd had insecurities with a parent. She'd had some with her ma too.

Ma had been a beautiful and wonderful mother. She hadn't always been perfect, but she'd set a good example in so many different ways—in her marriage and her adoration of her husband, in sacrificing for her family, and in her willingness to love and serve neighbors.

Even so, Clementine had wrestled with feeling that her ma had loved Clarabelle more than she'd loved her. Of course, Ma had probably loved them equally. She'd never done anything that could be construed as favoritism.

Yet Ma and Clarabelle had had similar temperaments and had both been soft-spoken and sweet. The two had gotten along very well and had a lot in common.

On the other hand, Clementine had always been louder and more strong-willed than her twin. At times, she'd felt as though she wasn't as likeable, that Ma was more interested in Clarabelle's life and activities. Clementine had always felt as though she had to work harder, talk louder, and do more to get Ma's attention.

Clementine's racing thoughts came to a halt. Was that why she'd loved spending so much time with Mrs. Worth? Because she hadn't felt as though she needed to compete with Clarabelle? Because Mrs. Worth had wanted to be with her and had always given her undivided attention?

And what if she'd sought out the attention of men as a way to make herself feel better? To make herself feel more loved and accepted and secure? She didn't know for sure, but this trip with Grady was teaching her that sometimes the hurts of the past came out in unexpected ways.

And sometimes the love came out in unexpected ways too.

She fell back against the mattress and stared up at the ceiling unseeingly, her body suddenly zinging with an energy and understanding she wanted to deny but couldn't. Did she still love Grady?

She wasn't sure if love could surface this quickly after she'd tried to bury it so deeply over the past years. But she did know she didn't want him to choose someone else to marry in order to win his dad's contest and start the hardware store. And she also knew she didn't want his dad to pick anyone else for Grady except her.

Grady had alluded to being okay with marrying her and had claimed she was too good for him. And he'd clarified that he wasn't against marrying her but just didn't want to use her to get the loan.

Maybe they still needed more time to restore their relationship and friendship. And maybe they would need time to let love truly develop between them. But if the attraction that was flaring to life was any indication, then it was obvious they both liked each other. And that was enough for now, wasn't it?

She didn't need him to profess his love. And maybe she didn't have to profess hers either.

In fact, if they got married tonight, maybe even right away, then the stalker wouldn't have any reason to keep pursuing her. She'd be a legally married woman and no longer available. Hopefully, once the stalker found out, he'd go away and leave them alone.

At the same time, Grady would win the contest with his dad and be able to get the loan for buying the building.

Overall, a hasty marriage would be the best option.

Now she just needed to convince Grady of the same thing.

18

Grady was so irritated with himself that he could hardly sit still. How had he let the stalker get away when he'd been that close in the restaurant?

Grady leaned forward in the chair next to Clementine's hotel room bed and braced his elbows on his knees. The churning in his gut told him the answer to his questions. He'd been so caught up in flirting with Clementine and all his feelings for her that he hadn't been paying attention to what was going on around them.

How could he have been so foolish? If he'd stayed alert, he would have realized someone was sitting at a table nearby, might have even gotten a look at the fellow's face.

As it was, the man was still unknown.

Grady glanced at Clementine's outline in the bed but then forced his attention back to the floor. He couldn't dwell on her being in the bed. He'd told himself that even before coming into her room. He had to think on other things tonight and not how much he wanted her.

But doing so was so hard. And honestly, it was becoming harder with every passing hour they were together.

It was his fault. All the *innocent* touches and all the *innocent* glances had just made him want her even more.

He buried his face into his hands and nearly groaned at the need welling inside him.

Of course, all day he'd been pretending to be engaged to her in order to prove that he and Clementine were in Georgetown to get married. It had been easy to fall into the role of her fiancé. And he'd been surprised at how much he'd liked it.

He'd also been trying to prove to Clementine that he knew how to flirt. While he wasn't really all that great at flirting, he'd had no trouble doing so with her.

Between the pretending and the proving, he'd let down his guard and given in to his longing for her. And now that his longing was roaming free, it couldn't be shoved back into the recesses of his heart and locked up again.

The trouble was keeping that longing from having too much leeway. He'd wanted to do much more than brush against her or give her meaningful looks once in a while. No, he'd wanted to wrap his arms around her and hold her close and kiss her senseless. But he couldn't. It was too much too soon.

"Grady?" Her tentative whisper broke through his internal ranting.

The whisper, just like everything about her, stirred emotion deep inside him, something that went beyond words.

"I have an excellent idea for tonight," she continued.

"No."

"How can you say no when you haven't heard it?"

"I can tell from the tone of your voice that I won't like it."

With a huff, she pushed up. "It's the best plan for both of us."

He already liked his plan for the fake wedding tomorrow. It wasn't foolproof, but it would hopefully help them identify and stop the stalker once and for all. But he knew he would listen to Clementine's plan anyway. In reality, it probably couldn't be much worse than his.

"Fine," he groused. "What's this excellent idea?"

"Let's get married tonight. Right away."

He snorted.

She remained quiet and unmoving on the bed.

His body stilled, and he allowed himself to look at her. "You're not serious, are you?"

She wasn't smiling and appeared almost grave. "I'm very serious. I've thought about it—"

"For what? A minute?"

"A few minutes."

"That's too big of a decision to make in a *few* minutes."

"Some of us don't need as long as others to make decisions."

"Marriage is a big deal, Clementine. And it's not something to rush into."

She grew silent again.

Maybe she was serious about it. But marriage hadn't been on his mind, except for the fake wedding. He'd expected to stand at the altar and talk until the stalker showed up. He hadn't planned on them saying any vows or doing any other part of the ceremony.

The real question was why she'd made the outlandish suggestion to really go through with it.

His heart began to tap an erratic rhythm. What if it wasn't outlandish?

"It's just something to consider, Grady," she said quietly. "We might not be in love with each other, but we're friends, and that's more than some married couples have."

They might not be in love? He knew he was in love with her and had been for a long time. So did that mean she didn't reciprocate?

A strange disappointment pricked his heart. He couldn't deny that he wished for her love. But he couldn't expect it right now and not any time soon. After the past few years of antagonism, it would take time and work to build her trust and respect and earn her love. But he was more than willing to take that time and do that work. And he could do that while they were married, couldn't he?

"Marriage will stop the stalker," she added. "And it will get you the loan from your dad."

"We can stop the stalker without marriage. And I already told you I don't want to use you to get the loan."

"I want to do it, Grady."

He shook his head. This was the part of her plan he didn't like—that she was sacrificing to help him and not because she loved him. The truth was, he didn't want her to marry him out of pity. He wanted her love.

Yet, what if he turned down her offer and then she never made it again? She might find someone else she cared about more than him. She never had a lack of interested men. And he didn't want to lose her. He'd never be able to stand back and watch her get married to someone else. And the other fact was that he'd never want another woman as much as he wanted Clementine.

He expelled a tight breath. "Are you sure marriage is what you want?"

"It's the best option for both of us."

"It's a permanent option."

"Well, I guess I can put up with you permanently."

The usual mirth was back in her voice.

He knew she was just trying to lighten the mood. She was good at that, and he appreciated that quality. But not at the moment, when he had to make sure she understood what she'd be getting herself into.

"If we really go through with getting married," he said in a grave voice, "our marriage won't be pretend."

"I understand."

"I want a real marriage."

"And I want a real marriage too."

"In *every* aspect."

"Of course—" Her reply ended abruptly, and she seemed to freeze.

He didn't say more. She had probably worked out the direction of the conversation. Even if the topic was a little embarrassing, he needed her to know that he wasn't remaining celibate in marriage.

"Are you saying you want to . . ." She didn't finish. Instead she just nodded. "You know."

"I'm saying I want to share the marriage bed with you."

She ducked her head, and he guessed that if he'd had light to see her features by, he'd have seen her face flushing.

The fact was, he was already attracted to her. Always had been, but even more so now that he'd just spent the day flirting with her. If they were living together as man and wife, his desire for her would only grow, he had no doubt. It was inevitable when she was the most beautiful woman God had ever created.

But while he had every intention of having a real marriage with a real marriage bed, he was also a patient man. He wanted her to want him too. More than that, he wanted her to love him in return.

In the end, her love was all that really mattered, and if he could win that, then he'd be a happy man.

"I'm not saying we have to sleep together right away." He spoke softly, hoping to reassure her. After all, if they did get married tonight, tomorrow, or some other date in the near future, they still needed time to adjust to each other. "We'll take things slowly and work at building our relationship first."

"Okay." Her answer was soft, almost shy.

"But at some point, we'll decide when to have more."

"That sounds fair."

The tension in his shoulders eased. He rolled them and leaned back in the chair.

"It makes sense that we'll need to eventually sleep with each other"—her voice dipped with embarrassment—"in order to have children."

"Yes." Suddenly he could picture her holding their baby, a big, strapping boy with his dark hair but her green eyes. How many children would they have? He hoped plenty. But even if they struggled to have children the way his parents had, he'd do his best not to neglect the blessings he already had. Maybe he'd do better.

She grew quiet again. Was she thinking about all that he'd revealed about his mom too? It was a reminder that they would see difficult days ahead at some point. Difficulties were inevitable in marriage. But if they committed to loving each other, they would make it through anything.

"Are you sure marrying me is what you really want?" he asked.

"I'm not just suggesting it because Clarabelle—all my siblings—got married this year and I don't want to be left behind, if that's what you're thinking."

"I wasn't thinking that." He shouldn't have taunted her and compared her with Clarabelle before. "I never should have brought it up. It wasn't fair."

"I also wasn't flirting more because I felt left behind."

"I wasn't thinking that either." Now that she was bringing up the issue, he guessed she had felt left behind, even if she was denying it. "But you should know that you being the last of your siblings to get married is my fault."

"What?" Her tone held humor again. "How could it be your fault?"

"Because I was an idiot to push you away as long as I did." He had been a big idiot. "If I'd never pushed you away, or even if I'd come to my senses sooner, we would have been married long ago."

"Is that right?" She was smiling. Although he couldn't see it, he could hear it in her voice.

"Yes, I'm right. I kept you from getting married, because obviously you were waiting for me to realize what an idiot I was."

"I wasn't waiting for you, and you're arrogant for saying so." She tossed her pillow at him again.

He easily caught it. "You've known all along that no other man can compare to me, which is why you were never interested in anyone else."

"See. Arrogant." She threw her second pillow, and it fell short of his chair.

"Just stating the facts."

She laughed lightly.

Relief seeped through him, and he lobbed both pillows back onto the bed. "Since we were destined to be together, I guess there's no reason to put it off any longer."

"Destined?"

"Absolutely."

She pushed off her covers to reveal her chemise, since she'd ruined her nightgown making bandages for him yesterday. "I guess I'll need to change into something more presentable."

A tremor of excitement pulsed into his blood. Was he really doing this? Getting married to Clementine?

"Do you think the reverend will be willing to come here tonight? It is rather late." She paused, kneeling in the middle of the bed. He could still see her hair spilling all around her, making her so achingly beautiful that he was glad the lantern was out, preventing him from losing his mind in one single glance.

"He's a friend of my dad's. He'll come." Grady couldn't keep a grin from spreading as he imagined standing in front of his dad in the living room, his arm around Clementine, declaring himself a married man and the winner of the challenge.

Now if only he could also win her love.

19

She was getting married.

Clementine peered into the mirror on the wall above the chest of drawers, brushed a wild strand of hair back into the hastily tied knot, then smoothed her hand down her wrinkled blouse and skirt.

Even though she'd taken the fresh clothing out of her bag and hung the items up when she was getting ready for bed earlier, she hadn't anticipated putting them on so quickly, and certainly not without ironing them. But she hadn't wanted to waste time with that. Not after Grady had knocked on her door a few minutes ago and told her the reverend had come right over and was now waiting downstairs.

She gave herself one last look, taking in her flushed cheeks and bright eyes.

She searched her face in the mirror, as if somehow she could find some sign of distress, hesitation, or a warning.

But she looked eager and even happy, like a bride about to marry the man of her dreams.

If she was honest about Grady, she knew he really was the man of her dreams. And maybe he'd been right a short while ago when he'd told her that she hadn't liked any other man because she'd been waiting for him. Maybe she hadn't been doing so consciously, but it was possible her heart had always known it belonged to Grady.

She pressed her hands against her cheeks to cool them off, then spun away from the mirror. Her gaze landed upon the unmade bed. After the mortifying discussion they'd just had about the marriage bed, she doubted he'd join her anytime soon.

As much as she'd enjoyed the closeness to him last night, she wasn't ready for anything more than simple holding, and she appreciated that Grady had indicated they would go slowly and build their relationship first.

At the very least, their marriage tonight would put an end to any gossip about his coming in and out of her room. He could sit by her bed as long and as often as he pleased once he was her husband.

Husband.

Grady Worth was about to become her husband. And she was about to become his wife.

She couldn't hold in a smile as she finished crossing the room. As she swung open the door, she halted at the sight of him leaning casually on one shoulder against the opposite wall, his feet crossed.

He'd changed into his suit, and now his dressy coat stretched across his shoulders as it always did. The white of his shirt contrasted with his tanned face and its layer of scruff. His dark trousers clung to his muscular legs. He'd even managed a tie and was as handsome in his suit as he was on the ice playing hockey.

His gaze swept over her. "You look beautiful."

At his sweet compliment, her heart melted. "You don't look so bad yourself."

He held out the crook of his arm, and she slipped her hand there, letting her fingers linger on his muscles a little too long.

"Are you ready for this?" he asked quietly as they started down the hallway.

Was she ready? For a life with Grady?

She loved being with him, loved how they could talk about anything, and loved how she could be herself with him. He never tried to impress her like other fellows did. He was always authentic. And he spoke the truth with her, even when it wasn't always pleasant.

They always had fun together. They enjoyed each other's company. And even when they fought, they still respected each other.

She couldn't think of any reason not to move forward with the wedding. "I'm ready. Are you?"

"I'm taking full advantage of your willingness tonight. I just hope you don't wake up in the morning and regret it."

"And why would I regret it?"

"Because you could have any man you want. So why me?"

At the top of the narrow stairway, she dragged him to a halt.

He was staring down the steps, and his hard jaw flexed.

"Grady Worth," she whispered. "You have always been and always will be one of my best friends. That's why I want to marry you. And because I can't think of a better man than you."

He slid her a sideways look, his eyes murky and dark.

The small look sent heat into her blood. She wasn't sure why such a brief glance affected her the way it did, except that he was so handsome and the look so sultry that it made her want to stop completely, press against him, and fuse her mouth to his.

She dropped her gaze away, hoping he couldn't read her wanton thoughts.

The fact was, no other man set her body ablaze like Grady did. No one even came close to affecting her the same way. That wasn't reason enough to marry him, but she couldn't deny she was happy that she'd get to look at him and claim his attention as much as she wanted from this day forward.

When they reached the bottom of the stairway, Mr. Curley, the hotel manager, paused his conversation with the reverend and grinned at them. An older man with slicked-back gray hair and a fleshy face full of wrinkles, he exuded a friendliness that had drawn Clementine from the moment she'd met him. "There's the happy couple right now."

A large-boned man in a tight suit stepped out of the sitting room and examined her with narrowed eyes. "So this is the woman?" His voice contained a heavy German accent along with a heavy dose of skepticism.

"Reverend, this is Clementine." Grady led her toward the two men. "Clementine, this is Reverend Ludwig."

She offered him a smile. "Thank you for coming tonight on such short notice, Reverend."

He didn't smile back but instead sniffed as he finished examining her. Then he pinned a severe look upon Grady. "You are certain your Vater is approving of this wedding?"

"I'm certain." Grady's lips cocked into a half grin. "My dad would have had me married to Clementine long ago if he'd had his way."

The reverend's severe expression remained hesitant.

"Don't worry, Reverend Ludwig." Mr. Curley waved them into the sitting room, which was cluttered with a mishmash of chairs and settees and overflowing bookshelves. Dimly lit by a lantern and the glow of the coal-burning fireplace, the room had a musty, old-book smell. "I've never seen Grady so enamored as I have today. It's obvious he loves Clementine."

Obvious? She arched a brow at Grady. The hotel proprietor had only been around them for a few minutes here and there throughout the day. How had he drawn that conclusion?

Grady shrugged, as if hearing her unasked question.

"Well, then." The reverend moved a chair out of his way before turning and facing them. "If Mr. Worth is approving this marriage, then who am I, his humble servant, to question him?"

She wasn't sure if the reverend was being serious, but as he began to open a worn book containing the order of worship, his expression remained solemn, and she had to bite back a smile.

She sensed Grady watching her, and when she met his gaze, his eyes were dancing with merriment. His humor only made it harder to contain her smile.

Reverend Ludwig cleared his throat. "In the name of the Vater, and of the Son, and of the Holy Ghost."

Mr. Curley made the sign of the cross and then gave a resounding "Amen."

The reverend waited and leveled a look at both her and Grady, as if waiting for them to say something.

"Amen?" she offered tentatively.

He sighed and then continued. "We are gathered here in the sight of God and of his Church to witness and bless the joining together of this man and this woman in holy marriage. This is an honorable estate, which God himself has instituted and blessed, and by which he gives us a picture of the very communion of Christ and his bride, the Church."

She was really doing this, getting married to Grady. A tremble wound through her.

Grady squeezed her hand, still in the crook of his arm.

As she glanced up at him, his eyes seemed to offer her assurance that if this wasn't what she wanted, she could say so and he'd put a stop to it.

She squeezed his hand back.

"The union of husband and wife in heart, body, and mind," Reverend Ludwig continued in his heavy accent, "is intended by God for their mutual joy, for the help and comfort given one another in prosperity and adversity, and, when it is God's will, for the procreation of children and their nurture in the knowledge and love of the Lord."

Had he really just mentioned the procreation of children as part of the wedding ceremony? She hastily dropped her gaze to the faded rug covering the floor. Talking about the issue had been embarrassing enough with just Grady, but it was all the more mortifying here and now.

Grady didn't seem to be paying attention and was

instead lifting his head and sniffing the air.

"Therefore," Reverend Ludwig said, "marriage is not to be entered into inadvisably or lightly, but reverently, deliberately, and in accordance with the purposes for which it was instituted by God."

Guilt pricked her. Were they entering marriage reverently? Especially since the decision had been so impulsive and hasty.

Grady spun away from her, breaking their connection. "Does anyone else smell that?"

The reverend slanted a severe gaze upon Grady. "Please do not interrupt—"

"It smells like smoke." Mr. Curley was sniffing the air now too.

Grady's brows furrowed. "Mr. Curley, did you leave something cooking in the kitchen?"

The older man cocked his head with an *are you serious?* look. "At ten o'clock at night?"

Clementine suddenly caught the waft of smoke too, and a light film of cloudiness seemed to be filtering into the room.

Without another word, Grady stalked across the room and through the door. Mr. Curley was right on his heels, and their steps echoed heavily in the hallway.

The reverend stood unmoving, his mouth hanging open as if he'd been about to say the next line of the ceremony and was now waiting for the men to return.

Clementine wasn't sure whether to stay with him or follow Grady.

Since she didn't want to bring the reverend's wrath down upon her, she decided to remain in her spot, but in the next instant, Grady's and Mr. Curley's shouts were echoing down the hallway.

"Fire! The hotel is on fire!"

20

Clementine raced through the hallway in the direction of the wafting smoke. As she reached the doorway of what appeared to be the kitchen, she stopped short at the sight of the rear wall covered in flames that were now swiftly spreading across the ceiling.

Grady was beating against the flames with a wet dishtowel, and Mr. Curley was throwing liquids upon it. The dishpan and a large kettle were already emptied and discarded on the floor, and now he had the coffee pot and was tossing the leftover contents onto the fire.

The splash of coffee that came out of the pot didn't do much to hinder the flames, and Mr. Curley scanned the kitchen frantically, his gaze landing on a jar of jelly on the worktable. He swiped it up, unscrewed the lid, then flung the contents onto the nearest portion of fire.

A glob flew out and hit the wall, but it did nothing to stop the momentum of the flames.

What could she do to help? They had to act quickly, or the fire might spread to other parts of the hotel.

With a sense of urgency rising inside her chest, she scanned the kitchen. There was another kitchen towel hanging on a peg near the back door. She started across the kitchen toward it.

"Stay out, Clementine!" Grady shouted with a sharp glare in her direction.

She shook her head. "We all need to help if we have any hope of putting out the fire."

"No." He stopped beating the flames, his forehead creased. "It's too dangerous. Now, get out of the building until the fire is out."

"Have her ask the other guests to exit with her," Mr. Curley called as he tossed another dollop of jelly into the flames. "Reverend Ludwig, would you go alert the fire chief?"

The reverend had obviously realized no one was coming back for the ceremony and had joined them in the kitchen. His eyes filled with fright as he watched the flames stretch to the ceiling.

She wanted to stay, but she suspected Grady would toss her over his shoulder and carry her out if she tried. And that would waste precious time needed to fight the fire. The next best thing to do was make sure the rest of the guests were safe.

From what she'd overheard Mr. Curley telling Grady

when they'd arrived earlier in the day, the hotel currently wasn't full. Hopefully that meant she could relay the word and give everyone plenty of time to get out of the building before the flames spread too far.

Thankfully the reverend seemed to see the urgency of the situation as well, and he hurried out of the building at practically a run. She raced up the stairs to the second floor and banged on doors, calling out the warning.

Within minutes, men in different stages of undress poured from the rooms. Only a few women were present and one family with two small children. As she explained what was happening, some of the men rushed down to aid in the kitchen while the rest gathered up what they could of their belongings and tromped down the stairs and outside.

Before going out, she peeked into the kitchen to check on Grady. He was busy shouting orders for the newcomers to form a water brigade out the back door to the well.

She quickly rounded up the others to assist with getting water, then headed to the backyard. As surrounding neighbors began to come out of their homes and businesses, they joined in, and soon they had a long line and were passing water from one person to the next as fast as they could from the well toward the hotel's kitchen.

It didn't take long for the fire department to arrive

with their engine and hoses in the back of a horse-drawn wagon. The volunteer firefighters were soon pumping water into the hotel kitchen and front hallway. Some of the volunteers had on black glazed-leather hats that set them apart from the rest of the men, but most wore ordinary clothing and hats.

She stood aside with the others on the edge of the yard, an alley and hillside behind them, and watched the men wrangle the long hoses. It didn't take long for the water to douse the flames, leaving big billowing clouds of smoke behind.

Near the back door of the hotel, Grady and Mr. Curley were calling out to the firefighters and directing them. She hadn't worried about Grady during the fire, knowing he was entirely capable of handling the disaster without getting hurt.

He'd shed his suit coat, and now his white shirt beneath his vest was covered in soot. His hair was damp and his face smudged, but he carried himself with authority and purpose, just like he always did.

He'd never looked better, and he was hers.

Her heart fluttered with a thrill. Grady Worth belonged to her.

As if he sensed her attention upon him, his gaze shifted her direction, landing upon her and assessing her all in one motion. He'd known right where she was, as if he'd been keeping his eye on her and watching over her.

She loved that no matter what he was doing, he was always there to take care of her. Not that she needed to be watched over. But she liked that he was protective.

She was getting married to him . . . had almost said her vows and pledged her life to him. Would they still be able to finish the ceremony tonight? She could admit she didn't want to have to wait until the morning.

No. She shook her head. She was being selfish. Of course they would have to wait. Even if the fire was out, a large portion of the hotel was in shambles, water and soot were everywhere, and they might not even be able to return to the hotel, depending on the extent of the damage.

Without her coat, the night air began to penetrate the sleeves of her bodice, especially now that she'd grown idle. A chill raced up her back, and she wrapped her arms over her chest and hugged herself.

Grady again glanced her way, taking note of her arms and probably realizing she was cold. He said something curt to the firefighter he was talking with and then broke away from the men, swiping up his coat from a barrel where he'd tossed it.

Warmth began to pool inside her. Not only was he watching over her, but he'd also noticed she was cold and was coming her way. If she didn't already love Grady, she would be falling in love with him soon.

At the calling of his name, he halted and pivoted.

Another firefighter was stepping out of the back door—a tall fellow someone had referred to as the fire chief. He beckoned to Grady, probably wanting him to come inside to assess the damage.

Grady hesitated, then handed his coat to Reverend Ludwig with a nod in her direction before he ducked through the blackened beams and into the burnt-out kitchen. The reverend was chatting with a group of men and didn't make a move toward her with the coat.

The others around her were already beginning to migrate toward the front of the hotel, probably hoping they could return to their rooms. She might as well retrieve the coat from the reverend and join everyone in front.

Or maybe she'd wait by the kitchen door for Grady to come back out.

Before she could make up her mind, a gloved hand captured her arm and began to tug her backward.

For a second, she was too surprised and confused to resist. Was someone pulling her farther from the danger?

As she twisted and caught a glimpse of a great coat with the collar pulled up and a derby hat tipped low, the confusion evaporated, and fear rushed in to take its place.

Her stalker had found her.

She opened her mouth to call out to the clusters of people moving away from her or to scream Grady's name, but another gloved hand snaked over her mouth, cutting off everything, even her next breath.

21

Smoke still hung heavily in the air.

Grady followed the chief firefighter through the blackened remains of the kitchen. Several other firefighters were slogging around in the inch of water that now covered the floor. They'd lit lanterns to illuminate the disaster as they searched to make sure all the sparks and flames were fully extinguished.

The walls were completely scorched, some down to the beams. The stove, the cooking ware, and the other supplies were likely too damaged to be of use again. The ceiling was blackened, and the floor above it was probably burnt too.

But as far as he could tell, the firefighters had managed to keep the flames from spreading to the second floor. From the stomping of heavy boots on the stairway and in the hallway above, he knew the other firefighters were checking the rest of the rooms to make sure everything was safe.

"It looks like most of the fire was contained to the back part of the hotel," the fire chief was saying as he crossed to the range that occupied half of one wall of the kitchen.

As Mr. Curley picked a long metal spatula out of the water on the floor, he shook his head at the charred remains of the handle. "What a disaster." He spoke the same words after every item he found.

"I know this is hard, Mr. Curley." Grady hated to think of the expense and effort it would take to rebuild. "But we can take heart that the rest of the hotel is mostly intact."

"True enough." The older man placed the metal spatula beside a charred coffee pot on top of the stove.

"And no one was hurt." Grady glanced to the open back door, hoping for a glimpse of Clementine, but he was at the wrong angle to see her where she'd been waiting with the other hotel guests. Hopefully the reverend had delivered his coat to her as he'd asked. It was too cold a night for her to be outside without some covering.

It was also too cold for everyone else, which was why he'd followed the fire chief inside. He wanted to do everything he could to speed up the cleanup efforts in order to allow the guests to return to the warmth of their rooms—or at least the rooms that were deemed safe.

"The fire destroyed most of the hallway outside the kitchen," the fire chief said, "but it didn't reach the steps or the sitting room. So I believe the front half of the hotel will be safe for people to use."

"But not the back rooms?" Mr. Curley's shoulders were slumped.

"At least not the couple of rooms above the kitchen."

The older man nodded. "I'll move the current guests into other rooms."

"Good." The chief grabbed one of the lanterns hanging from a post and lifted it above the stove. "I'll have the firefighters move everything they can out of those rooms."

"Thank you."

The fire chief bent and touched something behind the stove. "We didn't have to search too hard to find the source of the fire."

Grady had seen other businesses go up in flames over the years. It was one of the disadvantages that came from building with the timber that was so plentiful in the high country. Eventually the wood got old and became drier and more flammable. Brick was the way of the future, but it was more costly and difficult to cart up into the mountains.

"Did the stove malfunction?" Mr. Curley leaned in to examine the stove too. "Every once in a while, sparks fall out or go the wrong direction."

"Nothing like that." The fire chief's voice was grave. "I believe the fire was purposefully set."

A chill prickled Grady's neck. "Why do you think that?"

The chief lifted a small tin can from behind the stove. "Because of this."

Mr. Curley nodded. "Already told the chief I've never had any cans that size here in the kitchen. All of mine are larger."

Grady waited for the chief to continue explaining but could already guess what had happened.

The fire chief tipped the can over, and several charred matches fell into his gloved hand. "Someone dipped a rag in oil, stuffed it into the can, then placed the can behind the stove to make it look like the fire was an accident. It looks like it took him several tries before the fire started, then he tossed the matches into the can hoping the fire would burn up the evidence."

Mr. Curley bent in and examined the matches. "His plan didn't work."

The fire chief tossed the matches back into the can. "The fire in the can burned itself out before the matches were completely consumed."

"Who would do this?" Mr. Curley surveyed the disaster again. "And why?"

Grady's muscles tensed with a strange premonition. Had Clementine's stalker been responsible for starting the fire? What if he'd seen Reverend Ludwig coming to the hotel and realized the wedding was taking place tonight? And then what if he'd set the fire as a way to stop the wedding?

No, it wasn't possible. Surely the stalker wouldn't take things that far.

But even as Grady tried to deny it, his gut told him that's exactly what had happened.

"Blast," he said softly. He'd known the stalker was dangerous, but he'd never expected him to do something like set a fire and put other people's lives at risk.

The fire chief and Mr. Curley both shifted to look at him.

"I know who set the fire."

"Who?" Mr. Curley asked first.

"I don't actually know the identity of the person, but I do know someone followed Clementine and me to Georgetown hoping to keep Clementine from marrying me."

The fire chief's brows rose.

If the stalker had hoped to stop the wedding, that meant he was also lurking nearby, probably outside the hotel, watching the destruction unfold and hoping they'd all run out of the building. He might even be outside at the moment watching Clementine.

Suddenly Grady's blood turned cold. What if the stalker had set the fire not just to stop the wedding but also to flush them outside so that, amidst the chaos, he'd have a better chance at getting ahold of her?

With fear pounding through his body, Grady bolted toward the door, his footsteps slapping in the water. Clementine wasn't safe out there. She needed to come inside and stay by him.

Behind him, the fire chief called out another question, but he wasn't listening. The only thing he could think about was finding Clementine, picking her up, and holding her.

As he stumbled out the kitchen door into the darkness, he swept his gaze over the backyard and the alleyway and the hillside beyond. Only a few onlookers remained—a couple of firefighters, some neighbors, and a hotel guest or two.

He tried to slow his racing heart. Clementine was probably just with everyone else out front, making sure the others were okay, putting them at ease, and doing her best to be useful. She liked to be part of the action. That's just the way she was.

Sucking in a breath of fresh air to clear his lungs of smoke, he started toward the side of the hotel and the stone pathway that led to the street. As he picked up his pace, he scanned the groups ahead for her blond-red hair, her beautiful face, and her bright smile.

But as his gaze touched on each person and couldn't find her, his pulse only thudded faster.

At the sight of the reverend standing with one of the families, he called out. "Reverend Ludwig, did you give Clementine my coat?"

The large man regarded him severely before lifting his hand, revealing the coat draped across his arm.

A lump of dread landed in Grady's stomach. "Where is she?"

"I assumed she was with you."

Grady frantically searched the faces around him again. But she wasn't there.

Maybe she'd already gone inside?

He bounded up the front stairs toward a firefighter who was keeping people out. "Did you let my fiancée pass by? Long blond-red hair, green eyes, average height?"

The fellow shook his head. "Sorry, Mr. Worth. She didn't come this way."

He peered past the young man through the open front door that revealed the hallway with blackened wallpaper and charred rugs. "She didn't go inside?"

"No, sir. At least, not through the front door."

Maybe she'd gone in the back door while he'd been busy talking to the fire chief. "I'm going in to look for her." Grady didn't give the fellow a chance to protest and instead strode past.

Of course, no one would stop him—not when his dad owned the place and was well respected for his fair business practices.

Grady made a quick sweep of the hotel but didn't see her anywhere, and none of the other firefighters had come across her either. As he headed back outside, the dread inside only swelled. Maybe he'd missed her in the backyard. Maybe she'd been standing in the shadows. Maybe she'd gone to visit one of the neighboring businesses.

His mind raced to find a solution for where she might be. But as he reached the backyard and didn't see her anywhere, his heart told him the truth. The stalker had her.

22

Clementine wanted to scream, but the stalker's hand over her mouth was tight. And his glove also half covered her nose, so she was afraid she'd soon pass out from lack of air.

She'd already struggled to free herself, but he'd twisted her arm behind her back, so every misstep jarred her shoulder and arm painfully.

He'd led her along the alley past a line of businesses that were mostly closed. And he'd pulled her into a shadowed area once at the sound of nearing voices. As she'd waited, she'd planned to scream just as soon as the people were within sight. But no one had passed by, and she'd been left with little choice but to continue on with her captor.

She could see he was leading her toward the edge of town, and she knew she had to do something before they moved beyond the reach of light and help.

But what could she manage?

She'd craned her neck on multiple occasions, hoping to glimpse the fellow's face, but each time, the darkness of the night and the shadows of his hat had hidden him from view.

If only Grady hadn't gone inside. He'd been watching over her so well. Now he might not realize she was gone until it was too late.

At the sound of laughter ringing out from the open back door of a saloon ahead, the fellow pulled her against a building so they were out of sight.

For just an instant, his hold against her mouth slackened.

She ducked her head and freed her mouth. "Who are you and what do you want?" She managed the question before the stalker fumbled to cover her mouth again.

She dodged his hand. "Can we please talk?"

"No," he whispered. "Not until we-we're away from tow-town."

Even in a whisper, his voice had a familiar stutter.

"Elbert?" She dropped her voice now to a whisper.

He hesitated, as though he wasn't sure if he should admit who he was. But it was too late. She knew of only one man who had a stutter. Elbert Meriwether, Mrs. Meriwether's single son who lived with her.

"Elbert Meriwether, you release me this instant, do you hear?" She made her whisper as stern as possible.

He loosened his grip but didn't completely obey.

"I can't believe you of all people would resort to badgering a woman."

"I'm not bad-gering you."

"Yes, you are." She stomped her foot for emphasis. "You've been scaring me with your notes and spying and now this kidnapping."

"I didn't mean to bad-ger you."

"Well, you have." She broke away completely and spun to face him.

"I'm sor-ry." He tipped up the brim of his hat, revealing his balding head. His normally clean-shaven face was scruffy with the beginning of a mustache, but otherwise he looked like the normal Elbert she saw doing yardwork around town or helping his mother at the house. There was nothing sinister in his expression. His eyes were wide and expectant, as if he honestly thought she might be interested in him.

"Why are you doing all this to me, Elbert?" She tried to soften her voice, but she also had to be firm with him and make him understand that he couldn't keep harassing her.

"I'm ju-just trying to rescue you."

"Rescue me from what?"

"From Grady Worth." His gaze darted around the alley as though he expected Grady to barrel toward them and knock him over.

"I don't need rescuing from Grady."

"But you-you don't like him. You said so."

Her ready chastisement faltered. She had disparaged Grady plenty of times. She'd made no secret of the fact that she disliked him to anyone who would listen. She might have even complained to Mrs. Meriwether a time or two about Grady. Perhaps Elbert had overheard her.

"That's why I-I started the fire to-night."

"You started it?"

He nodded as though he'd done a heroic act in burning the hotel. "I'm stop-ping him from marry-ing you. And you-you can mar-ry me instead."

Her heart dropped with the sudden realization of what had happened. Because she'd complained about Grady so much, Elbert really did think he was coming to her rescue. He probably thought Grady was forcing her into marriage, and he'd left Breckenridge to chase after her in order to help her.

"I l-love you-you." Elbert spoke the words solemnly, his expression earnest.

They were words she wished she could hear from Grady instead. And she could no longer deny that she loved him. Here, with Elbert professing his love, she knew without a doubt she would always love Grady.

But clearly she'd given Elbert the wrong signals—as she'd probably done to other men—and now she would have to set him straight about their relationship and probably hurt his feelings in the process.

"Were you the one giving me the gifts last week?"

He nodded.

"That was nice of you, Elbert, but you shouldn't have—"

"But you-you gave me candy first, and I-I was trying to be nice."

She halted and calculated the passing of time. Yes, his gifts had started the day after she'd taken Mrs. Meriwether and him candy almost two weeks ago.

"And the roses and the notes?" she asked. "Those were also from you?"

"I wanted to give you-you real roses," he said in his slow and stuttering voice. "But it's not the seas-son."

In the light coming from the saloon down the alley, she could see that Elbert's expression was sincere. He hadn't meant to threaten her or make her feel unsafe. He wasn't a vicious man, and he certainly wasn't dangerous. She doubted he owned a gun or even knew how to work one.

No, instead, he'd thought she liked him because of her gift, and he'd just been trying to protect her from Grady.

She crossed her arms, the cold finally penetrating through her fear, making her realize she was still coatless and freezing. And she needed to get back to the hotel before Grady started to worry about where she was.

Even so, she had to apologize to Elbert. "I'm sorry for confusing you, Elbert. But I do love Grady, and I want to get married to him."

Elbert's brows rose. "But you-you said you loathe him."

Her mind went back to the conversation she'd had with Grady just a few days ago when she'd made this week's delivery to Mrs. Meriwether. Grady had been with her, and Elbert had watched them bickering again. And she *had* told Grady she loathed him.

"Grady and I have had a complicated relationship." She didn't want to go into all the details. It would take too long to explain and wasn't anything Elbert needed to know. "But we've worked things out, and we care about each other."

Elbert studied her face.

"You're my friend, Elbert, but I'll never care about any other man the way I care about Grady." There, she'd said it, and she crossed her fingers that Elbert wouldn't be too upset.

He watched her another moment before his shoulders slumped. "So you-you won't mar-ry me?"

After all she'd just said, did he really think she'd want to? She bit back the sarcasm and gentled her tone. "I can't. I want to marry Grady."

At a shout from down the alley, Elbert spun, his eyes widening at the sight of a familiar form running toward them.

Grady had come after her.

"Are you okay?" he called, worry ringing in his voice.

"I'm fine." And she really was.

As Grady thundered closer, he took in Elbert standing beside her, and surprise flashed across his face. Then his expression hardened. "Elbert Meriwether, I never would have guessed you were the one stalking Clementine."

"Stalk-ing?" His voice squeaked as if he had no idea what the word meant.

"If you've hurt Clementine, I'll kill you."

Elbert held out his hands as if to stop Grady from reaching him. He stumbled backward and almost tripped and fell, but then he righted himself quickly before spinning and beginning to run.

23

Rage burned in Grady's gut. Even if Elbert hadn't hurt Clementine, Grady wanted to kill him. Maybe not literally, but he wanted to teach him a lesson he wouldn't soon forget.

Elbert's heavy, flat footsteps slapped against the gravel as he raced away.

Grady's long legs easily ate up the distance, so within seconds he was grabbing Elbert's coat and dragging him to a stop.

When Grady had entered the alley a few minutes ago, he hadn't known which way to go. He'd decided on the route that would lead a stalker out of town more quickly, and now he was glad he had. It hadn't taken him but half a minute to see the two in the distance with the light from the nearby saloon illuminating them.

As he'd drawn closer, he'd realized the stalker wasn't holding Clementine. They'd appeared to be talking. And as soon as he'd recognized the stalker was Elbert Meriwether, he'd stuffed his revolver back into his holster and instead readied his fist.

"Don't hurt him, Grady." Clementine's tone chastised him.

From everything he'd been able to assess as he'd neared her, she hadn't been harmed in any way except that she was still coatless and cold. But he wasn't listening to her right now. He was too mad.

He yanked Elbert to a stop.

The fellow yelped.

Grady spun him around and then threw a punch. His knuckles connected with Elbert's cheek and nose.

"Grady Worth!" Clementine shouted behind him. "I told you not to hurt Elbert!"

Elbert had closed his eyes and was cringing, clearly preparing himself for another hit. Blood was already flowing from his nose down his mouth and chin.

The man deserved at least one more hit for the way he'd terrorized Clementine, didn't he? And it would certainly teach him that Clementine was Grady's and that Elbert had better not look at her again—not even sideways.

"Let him go." Clementine was hauling on the back of Grady's vest, but even as she did so, he could feel her shaking. He didn't know whether it was from the cold or from everything that had happened. All that mattered was getting her inside and warmed up.

Grabbing the front of Elbert's coat, he pressed his face close. "Don't you ever come near Clementine again, do you hear me?"

Elbert gulped, then nodded.

"She's mine." He practically roared the words, but he didn't care. The more people who knew that Clementine was his woman, the better. "Mine."

Elbert nodded again.

Grady straightened but didn't let go of Elbert's coat.

Clementine had cocked her head and was watching him with a scowl. "If you're done acting like a barbarian, maybe I can explain what happened."

"We're getting you inside first." He drew Clementine into the crook of his body but at the same time kept a one-handed grip on Elbert, dragging him along as he hurried them down the alley back toward the hotel.

Of course, Clementine didn't wait to share her explanation. Instead, she told him the details of what had transpired. Elbert readily confessed to the stalking, including taking an extra key from the general store so that he could let himself in whenever he wanted.

"It's all my fault," Clementine said as Grady led her through the front door of the hotel after handing Elbert off to one of the firefighters with the instructions to hang on to him tightly and not let him sneak away.

"What Elbert did was wrong." Grady guided her into

the sitting room, which was untouched by the fire and now mostly cleared of smoke with the windows open.

She was still tucked against his body. "He wouldn't have done any of it if I hadn't given him that box of candy to begin with."

"That's not true, Clementine." He swiped up the knitted blanket draped over the nearest wingback chair. "Elbert has obviously cared about you for a long time, and he was just biding his time for the right moment to express it."

"But I should have been more careful about leading him on and making it seem like I was interested. You were right about it all."

He crossed to the nearest window and began to close it. "A lot of what I said about your flirting was because I was jealous." He could feel her eyes on him, watching his every move with an interest that would have sent heat shooting through him if he weren't still too mad at Elbert and too scared by the thought of what could have happened to her if it had been anyone else more dangerous.

"What I'm trying to say"—he finished closing the first window and then moved to the second—"is that a woman's friendliness, even when it's too flirty, is never an excuse for a man to disrespect her."

"I still had—have—a responsibility not to lead men on."

"I won't argue with you about that. But Elbert should have talked to you instead of hiding behind his notes and fake flowers."

"Maybe with his stutter, talking is hard."

"Having courage is hard too, but necessary." With the windows pulled down, Grady turned his attention to the stove.

Clementine huddled beneath the blanket in the middle of the room, still shaking and still watching him, her forehead creased with worry. "What should we do with Elbert? Should we talk to him and then send him home?"

Grady knelt beside the coal bin. "As soon as I'm done here, I'm taking him over to the sheriff's office and having him locked up in jail."

"No, Grady. That's not necessary—"

In the process of opening the stove door, Grady paused and leveled what he hoped was a severe look upon her. "He started a fire in the hotel."

She opened her mouth to say more, but then pursed her lips and nodded.

"He put many lives in danger tonight with his recklessness." Not to mention he'd kidnapped Clementine. And that was in addition to all the stalking, including the note with the death threat. Long-term, maybe Elbert would be fine and realize he'd made mistakes. But in the short term, Grady had no choice but to make sure the fellow wasn't able to cause more problems.

Grady added fuel to the fire, stoked the flames, then situated Clementine in a chair close to the warmth. She was somber and didn't say much as he left the room.

He retrieved Elbert and then headed down the street to the sheriff's office, where the jail was located. Of course, with the fire having caused a commotion, the sheriff was awake and milling about on Main Street. At the sight of Grady with Elbert in tow, he crossed over and wasted no time in taking Elbert inside and locking him in the one and only cell.

Grady relayed the events of the past two weeks as the sheriff recorded the details. Of course, Grady left out the part about faking the engagement to Clementine. As far as he was concerned, their engagement was real.

The trouble was, now that they'd discovered who the stalker was, they didn't need to get married so hastily. In fact, they didn't need to get married at all.

As Grady finally left the sheriff's office and stepped out into the November night, he expelled a tight breath and peered up at the black sky. Stars covered the expanse, revealing the imposing mountain peaks that rose all around the town.

What should he do?

Even though his heart tapped out a need for Clementine that would never go away and could never be denied, he also knew that they wouldn't have been considering marriage right now, or even a relationship, if they hadn't been facing danger. And now that the danger was gone, he didn't want to pressure her.

Maybe it was best if they returned to Breckenridge and had time to court properly. He could work at winning over her heart so that when they finally did get married, she would be doing it because she loved him, not because she felt coerced.

Yes, he knew she was attracted to him to a degree. There was no denying the heat that flared between them. But attraction was different from love. And he wanted her love. If he was really honest with himself, he'd been wishing for it for years. A little more time wouldn't matter, would it?

Waiting was the right thing. There would be no wedding tonight.

He lowered his head and tried to fight off the disappointment that crowded against him.

24

A gentle prodding woke Clementine. She opened her eyes to find Grady slipping his arms underneath her and lifting her from the chair, where she'd dozed in the hotel sitting room. His face was still smudged with soot, the coyote scratch red, his dark hair messy, his white shirt streaked. But somehow he still managed to look entirely too appealing.

"Grady." Her voice came out sleepy, and she didn't resist as he settled her against him. Instead, she snuggled closer, loving the feel of his arms surrounding her and the solidness of his chest.

A glance at the mantel clock told her that the time was well past midnight and he'd been gone for over an hour.

Shortly after he'd left, the hotel guests had been admitted back into their rooms. The firefighters had still been working with Mr. Curley in the kitchen, helping to sweep out the water and board up the spots that needed patching to keep out the elements and wild creatures. She'd offered to assist, but Mr. Curley had shooed her back into the sitting room, insisting that she wait there for Grady.

With firm footsteps, Grady carried her toward the door.

She stifled a yawn. "Where are we going?"

"I'm taking you up to bed."

"No, put me down."

He kept walking. Of course.

She wriggled against him. "Grady Worth, I'm not going anywhere until we're married."

At her declaration, his steps came to an abrupt halt, and he stared straight ahead, his jaw flexing.

She struggled to free herself from his arms, and he finally placed her gently on her feet. She rounded on him. "We are still getting married tonight, aren't we?"

His jaw was still clamped together stubbornly, giving her the answer.

"Why not?" She could admit she'd been looking forward to his return and to finishing their wedding. When she'd drifted to sleep, the reverend had even still been at the hotel, his loud German accent rising above the others in the kitchen. He'd probably been waiting for Grady's return just like she had.

Grady heaved a sigh, one laced with weariness.

Maybe he was too tired after all that had happened. "We can keep the ceremony brief if you're worn out."

"That's not it."

"Then what?"

He rubbed a hand across his jaw. "Listen, Clementine. With Elbert in jail, we don't need to rush this—"

"We're not rushing."

"Yes, we were. To keep you safe."

"No." Her heart began to thud hard in protest. He was right, but she didn't want to admit it, didn't want to lose him, didn't want to let him get away now that she had him again.

He blew out a breath. "We'll go back home to Breckenridge and give ourselves more time to make sure this is what we both want."

"What if I don't want more time?" She fisted her hands on her hips and glared at him.

He backed up. "We need it."

"You need it."

"We both do."

"I think I know what I want." She huffed and stamped her foot. She didn't care if the move was childish. She was irritated at him. "And I want to marry you. Tonight."

The dark brown of his eyes was murky with emotions she couldn't name but which sent strange spirals of heat through her.

He wanted her too. She could see it in his eyes. She'd thought he was ready earlier. So why was he holding back now?

She took a step toward him.

He stiffened.

"Don't do this, Grady," she whispered, closing the gap with another small step.

"Do what?" he whispered back.

"Push me away without talking about the issues." She didn't know how she could survive losing him again—not after opening up her heart and letting herself love him so quickly.

He seemed to swallow hard.

She reached him and took both of his hands within hers. "You're the one who told me that having courage is hard but necessary. So have courage, and tell me why you're pushing me away."

He stared at her hands surrounding his.

He was going to reject her again. She could feel it. Maybe she'd been wrong to think that their relationship could grow into something stronger. Maybe all they would ever be was friends.

She had the urge to shove past him and run up to her room, where she could be alone with her misery. She started to let go of his hands, but he gripped her fingers tighter.

"Wait." His voice held a soft plea.

She let her hand sink back into his.

"You're right. Maybe I am trying to push you away. But only because I don't want you to feel obligated to go through with the marriage."

She caressed his hand, unable to stop herself. "I don't feel obligated any more now than I did earlier."

He caressed her hand back, his long fingers drawing a line across hers. "The thing is . . ."

She watched his face, trying to read his expression but unable to see anything but his hesitation.

"The thing is . . ." He started again, then sighed.

She waited quietly and stroked his fingers once more, even though her insides were churning.

He lifted his eyes and met hers. "I love you, Clementine. I have for a long time."

Tears sprang to her eyes. "Really?"

"Yes, really. I've been wishing for your love in return. And now I want to wait to get married until you have the chance to catch up to me and fall in love with me too."

A lump formed in her throat, and she was too impatient to push the words out past the swell of emotion. Instead, she threw her arms around him and lifted onto her toes, pressing her lips against his.

She didn't wait for him to respond to her but instead kissed him deeply with all the desperation and need and love that filled her.

He paused for only a second before snaking his arms around her, pulling her flush, and letting his lips fuse with hers. He opened up the kiss so that it was as wide and deep as the mountain valleys, transporting her there and to the mountain peaks all in one swift move.

This. With his kiss. In his arms. Against his body. This was where she wanted to live the rest of her life. If she never had to go anywhere else, she would die a very happy woman. She could kiss him all day long and all night and never tire of it.

His hand at her back slipped to her hip and tightened there possessively. He hadn't rejected her. Instead, he'd claimed her with his love. He loved her. In fact, he'd said he'd always loved her.

Just like she'd always loved him . . .

She broke the kiss and then took a rapid step away from him.

His fingers lingered on her waist and slid up her arms, and his eyes were even darker, desire raging there—a desire that threatened to pull her back and keep kissing her.

And oh, she wanted to keep kissing him. And this time she would glide her fingers across his shoulders to his face and there explore the scruff and the tautness of his jaw and maybe plunge her fingers into his hair.

But first . . .

She pressed a hand against his chest to stop him.

Beneath her hand, she could feel the rapid beating of his heart. "Grady?"

His gaze dropped to her mouth, and she could almost hear his thoughts about ravaging her lips.

She nearly threw herself back against him to let him do as he wanted with her. But she knew she needed to clarify something first.

"Grady?" she said softly again.

He tore his attention from her mouth and lifted his gaze to hers. The desire and love there took her breath away.

"I want you to know," she managed a whisper, "I've been wishing for your love for a long time too."

His brows quirked in question.

"What I mean is that I love you already. I might have even fallen in love with you when I first met you years ago."

"So, are you telling me we've both been in love with each other all this time?"

"Yes, but we were too stubborn to admit it."

A small smile worked at his lips. "Do you think everyone else knew except for us?"

She smiled in return. "Probably."

He started to angle down, his eyes full of a heat that promised another passionate kiss. His lips barely had time to brush hers before a cough came from the doorway.

She startled and broke away from Grady.

"Mr. Worth, I have been waiting for your return," came the strong German accent of Reverend Ludwig.

Grady didn't let Clementine get but a step away before he snagged her arm, stopping her, his eyes still on her mouth.

He wasn't thinking about kissing her in front of the reverend, was he?

As though hearing her unasked question, he nodded.

She shook her head in response and then turned her attention to the reverend. "You're here to finish the wedding?"

He frowned and held up Grady's coat. "I came to return this."

"And finish the wedding," she insisted, then before Grady could protest, she dragged him toward the reverend.

She held Grady's arm, keeping him in place. Not that he was fighting against her, thank goodness. "I think you were just about to have us state our vows."

Reverend Ludwig's forehead creased into the beginning of a frown. "We do not have our witness—"

"I'm right here," Mr. Curley announced as he stepped past the reverend into the room. He was full of soot, his gray hair standing on end and his clothing soaked in places. But he smiled at them anyway. "Let's get these two married before they combust and cause another fire." He winked at them.

At the bold insinuation, the flush in her face turned hotter.

Grady cast her a sideways look, his lips turning up into a smirk.

She loved his smirk and everything about him, but she released a huff. "Let's do this before Grady decides to make me wait any longer."

The reverend glanced between the two of them for a moment before gathering his book from the table in the hallway and returning. He opened it and cleared his throat. "We are gathered here in the sight of God and of his Church to witness—"

"We don't need to redo everything." Grady's voice was sharp and impatient.

"But we must do things properly—"

"Just the vows," Grady growled.

The reverend hesitated only a moment longer before skimming down the page of his order of service.

Clementine bent her head to hide her smile. Oh, she loved her man. With him, her life would never be dull. She had no doubt they would clash again plenty of times and have fights and disagree, since they were both so stubborn and strong-willed. But they were both equally determined and passionate. And together, they would face life's joys and challenges and continue to become better and stronger in the process.

"Will you have this woman to be your wife," the

reverend continued, "to live with her in holy marriage according to the Word of God? Will you love her, comfort her, honor her, and keep her in sickness and in health and, forsaking all others, be husband to her as long as you both shall live?"

"I will." Grady's voice was strong and certain.

Emotion rose swiftly inside her again. She'd given up on wishing for this moment. And now here she was, marrying the man she loved.

Reverend Ludwig shifted to face her. "Will you have this man to be your husband, to live with him in holy marriage according to the Word of God? Will you love him, comfort him, honor him, obey him, and keep him in sickness and in health and, forsaking all others, be wife to him as long as you both shall live?"

"I will." She spoke without hesitation and smiled up at him as she did so.

His eyes filled with a happiness that spilled over into her.

"I love you." She couldn't contain the words.

He bent and touched his lips to hers, showing his love in return with a passion that ignited fresh heat inside her.

"No, no, no." The reverend's objection sounded a million miles away. "I have not yet pronounced you man and wife."

Grady broke the kiss, leaned his forehead against hers, and then grinned. "Go ahead, Reverend. I'm giving you five seconds, then I'm kissing my bride again."

Mr. Curley chuckled.

The reverend spoke rapidly and loudly, clearly trying to finish the ceremony before Grady carried through with his kiss. "Now that Grady and Clementine have consented together in holy marriage and have given themselves to each other by their solemn pledges, and have declared the same before God and these witnesses, I pronounce them to be husband and wife, in the name of the Vater and of the Son and of the Holy Ghost."

The words were barely out before Grady's mouth descended on hers again, eagerly.

Joy swelled within her. She'd gotten everything she'd wished for and so much more.

25

"I don't like surprises, Grady." Clementine's stomach fluttered with excitement as Grady led her blindfolded through the fresh snow toward the general store. "You know that."

Grady stopped her in the middle of the alley, the chill of the morning swirling around her. One of his arms was around her waist. "Liar." His whisper was sultry and echoed in the hollow of her ear, and in the next instant his mouth pressed in hard.

She couldn't hold back the gasp or the tremble to her knees.

She slid her hand to his chest and grasped his shirt to keep from buckling. Even after the past week of being married, she couldn't get used to his kisses and the power they wielded over her. Just a kiss to her ear had the ability to render her senseless.

During the rest of their stay in Georgetown for a few

days, they'd done lots and lots of kissing, but Grady had only held her at night the same way he had that night in the mine cavern.

When they'd returned to Breckenridge and told his dad they were married, his dad had gloated. "Just what I predicted," he'd said before he'd started hoisting boxes of already packed belongings across the alley and up into the spare room above the store.

In fact, while they'd been gone, he'd already started moving some of his own clothing over. He'd been that certain they'd return married. And he'd been right.

He'd already had his dinner with Mrs. Meriwether and determined that she wasn't the one for him, which was probably a good thing after all that had happened with Elbert. When Mrs. Meriwether had learned about her son's crimes, she'd closed up her home and traveled to Georgetown to live near Elbert as he awaited a trial.

Meanwhile, Mr. Worth had made contact with Mrs. Raleigh, the widow with three children, and seemed to be enjoying getting to know her. In any case, he wanted Clementine and Grady to have the home and said it belonged to them now.

That first night she'd slipped into the bed in their home, she'd welcomed Grady's embrace from behind, the same way she had the previous nights.

As he'd settled in with his arms around her, using tender restraint and showing her that he loved her more than he loved himself, she'd known then that she was more than ready to share everything with him, including the marriage bed.

She'd slowly turned over so that she was facing him, then she'd kissed him and let that kiss tell him of her desire for more.

Now, with his kiss against her ear, longing pulsed low in her stomach, and she was tempted to rip off the blindfold, spin Grady around, and march him back inside the house. But they'd already lingered longer than usual that morning, almost to the point that she'd begun to suspect Grady was delaying her.

Then, when they'd stepped out of the house, he'd slipped a neckerchief around her eyes and told her he had a surprise for her.

"Tell me what you're doing." She clung to him and lifted her face to his, hoping he'd take her hint and bend down and kiss her.

In the next instant, his lips meshed with hers. With the chill of the snowy morning, his lips were especially warm and delicious against hers, and she was hungry for him again—a hunger that was embarrassingly frequent. Thankfully, his hunger for her was just as intense.

"Come on now, you two!" Mr. Worth's laughter rang across the distance. He'd happily agreed that Grady had won their contest and had loaned Grady the money to buy the building next door to the store that same day.

Grady had gone over and spoken to the pharmacist right away, and Clementine was more than pleased for Grady, especially after being in Georgetown and realizing how important it was to him to be able to make his own way and find his own success independent of his dad. She was proud of him and knew that he'd one day be a prosperous businessman just like his dad.

"You can kiss later," his dad called, his voice tinged with laughter.

Grady broke their kiss. "Talk about impatient."

She smiled at the prospect of the day ahead. If it was like the past couple, she and Grady would be constantly making up excuses to visit each other. Yesterday, she'd counted at least a dozen visits from him, most of them in the back room of the store, where he'd kiss her desperately for as long as possible before sneaking back out and crossing over to the livery.

She'd visited him several times to give him candy samples, hoping to steal kisses from him too. But they didn't have any privacy there, although on one occasion they'd stepped into a stall and kissed for a minute before his assistant had caught them.

Grady's hold around her body was gentle as he guided her ahead, but instead of going through the back door of the store as she'd expected, he veered away.

"Where are we going?" she asked.

He chuckled. "You'll see soon enough."

"Grady Worth, you're terrible."

"Clementine Worth, you're terrible too."

She loved the sound of her married name. She halted again, and this time she was the one to swivel around, letting her hands roam until they found his scruffy cheeks and pulled him down for a kiss—a kiss that consumed her and made her forget all about the rest of the world so that she and Grady were the only two who existed.

Another laugh wafted through the chilly morning, this one belonging to her brother Maverick. "You weren't kidding when you said all they do is kiss."

"Can't keep them apart." Mr. Worth chortled. "With all those years of pent-up feelings, my guess is they'll be doing lots more kissing for quite a while."

Embarrassed heat rushed through Clementine. But more than that, she was surprised that Maverick was in town so early in the morning on a weekday.

Clementine broke away from Grady and pulled off her blindfold to find herself at the rear entrance of the pharmacy. Mr. Worth, Maverick, and Hazel stood just inside the back of the shop. Her handsome brother with his dark hair and blue eyes had his arm around Hazel, who was just as pretty as always with her glowing face and rounded stomach, her pregnancy beginning to show.

The three were smiling as Clementine stepped through the door. She gave Maverick and Hazel hugs, not having seen them yet since she'd returned from

Georgetown as a married woman.

"It's about time," Maverick said as he released her and stepped back, offering her one of his crooked grins.

"That's what I said." Mr. Worth stood beside Grady, the two of them watching her expectantly. Too expectantly.

Grady gave a pointed look at the tall table in the center of the room. There, in the middle of the table, were the boxes of candy she'd made yesterday and had ready to either deliver or display.

Then Grady nodded at the shelves on the opposite wall. They were filled with all her candy-making supplies: bowls, knives, molds, pans, and more.

Her heartbeat came to a rapid halt. "What's all of this doing here?"

She glanced around to find cutting boards, oven mitts, a utensil holder filled with wooden spoons, and even pretty towels hanging from hooks near the sink. Most of it looked brand new, never used, and it was all arranged so beautifully.

"I don't understand," she started.

Grady laced his fingers through hers and then began to tug her excitedly to the door that led to the front room. As he stepped inside, he covered her eyes with his hands.

"What are you doing, Grady?" Her voice trembled as understanding of his surprise began to sink in.

"I'm making your dream come true," he whispered as

he dropped his hand away and let her take in the freshly painted interior, including all the wall shelves—a mixture of white, pink, and red. Not only were the shelves and walls and even the window trim painted, but the glass displays were polished to a shine and filled with her candy. More jars and containers lined the top of the counters, and they were also brimming with colorful varieties of candy—some that she'd made and others that had been purchased.

Maverick, Hazel, and Mr. Worth had followed them into the store and were all three beaming as they watched her.

She could only gape, too overwhelmed to speak.

"My dad and Mrs. Raleigh were here yesterday organizing the place," Grady explained quickly. "And Hazel and Maverick came in early and set up the kitchen."

"Really?" She wanted to rush over to them and hug them all, but Grady was still showing her everything, and she was trying to take it in.

"One night after closing, we hired a crew of workers to paint," he was saying. "If you don't like the colors, we can have them come back and change them—"

She turned and silenced him with a quick and happy kiss. "I love it." It truly was everything she'd ever dreamed of in a confectionery of her own. In fact, it was more than she'd dreamed of.

Except that in fulfilling her dream, he'd sacrificed his.

"But, Grady." She grabbed his coat. "You bought this place for your hardware store. What will you do now?"

He shrugged. "I didn't have my heart set on having a hardware store. It was just a means to expand. And I'll still have plenty of opportunities to do that."

"But the cost of the building. I can't—"

"We're in this together. Partners."

She nodded, relieved he hadn't tried to give it to her. He clearly knew that she wouldn't have accepted such a gift, but she could accept that they were business partners.

Her gaze swept over the beautiful interior of her new shop and the name Clementine's Confectionery painted in pretty pink letters on the window.

She couldn't hold back her squeal of delight as she launched herself against Grady.

He caught her, his grin making a rare appearance—although she'd seen more and more of them lately, so many that she hoped they would no longer be so rare.

He wrapped his arms around her, and she did the same to him. "Thank you, Grady. But you know you didn't have to do this."

"I know." He pressed a kiss against her head. "But there's nothing I want to do more than spend the rest of my life making each of your dreams come true. Whatever those might be."

She closed her eyes, contentment pulsing through her.

She didn't deserve this man or his love. And she didn't deserve all that he was doing for her.

But she'd wished for him and his love anyway. And sometimes wishes happened to come true.

Dear Reader,

Well, that's a wrap! Clementine and Grady finally got their love story, and now the Oakley family saga is complete. I hope you enjoyed the enemies-to-lovers trope, which is always a tricky one to write with the right balance of angst and attraction.

So, you might be asking, what's next? (I hope you are!) I'm happy to report that I'll be returning to Summit County in the Colorado Rockies, but this time to the Noble Ranch! Do you remember Sterling Noble from Maverick and Hazel's story in Book 1 (he was Maverick's best friend and Hazel's older brother)? After having his bride, Violet Berkley, run away on their wedding day, Sterling has sworn off love and marriage. But of course, when Violet comes back into his life, he can't keep his love for her buried—even though he tries very hard!

Join me for more romance and adventure with another Western series that involves the Noble family as each of the siblings navigates the winding journey to find love.

As always, I love hearing from YOU! If you haven't yet joined my Facebook Reader Room, what are you waiting for!? It's a great place to keep up-to-date on all my book releases and book news, as well as a fun place to connect with other readers and me.

Farewell, but not for long!

Make sure you didn't miss out on any other books in the High Country Ranch series. Here's a complete list of all the books. They can be read as standalones, but they're even better read in order.

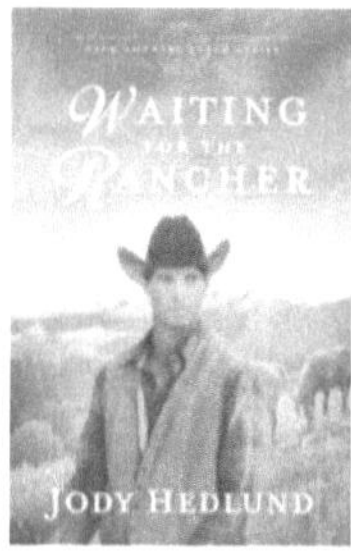

Waiting for the Rancher

Hazel Noble loves her job managing the mares at High Country Ranch. As the foaling season begins, she gets to spend even more time with the horses . . . and with her secret crush, Maverick Oakley, the owner of High Country Ranch and her brother Sterling's best friend. When Maverick unwittingly ruins Sterling's wedding, he goes from best friend to worst enemy. With the rift between their families, Maverick is faced with the possibility of losing Hazel, and he can no longer deny how much he's always cared about her.

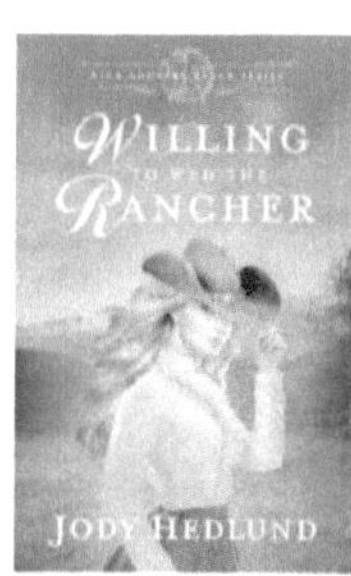

Willing to Wed the Rancher

Assistant schoolteacher Clarabelle Oakley has a hard time saying no. When Eric Meyer, widowed father of two of her young students, proposes to her, she botches her effort to tell him no and that she wants to marry for love, not convenience. Only days later, the unthinkable happens, and Clarabelle learns she's been given charge of Eric's children and his farm. Professor Franz Meyer arrives in Summit County, Colorado, to make peace with his estranged brother but discovers Eric is gone, leaving too many unanswered questions.

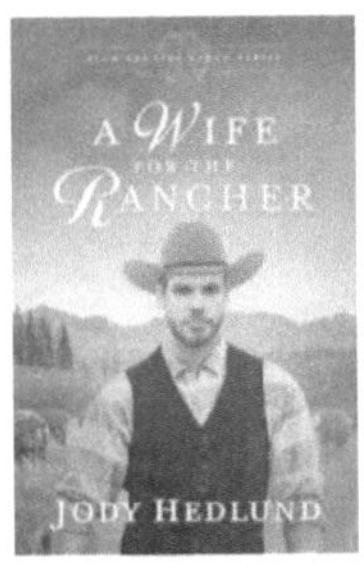

A Wife for the Rancher

Millionaire heiress, Genevieve Hollis, has everything she wants except one thing, freedom, because her guardian stepmother insists on overseeing every move she makes. When Genevieve sees a newspaper advertisement from a rancher seeking a mother for his baby, she jumps at the chance to escape. Ryder Oakley has suffered the repeated misfortune of losing the people he loves most, so now that he's a single father with a newborn baby, he's determined not to lose his son.

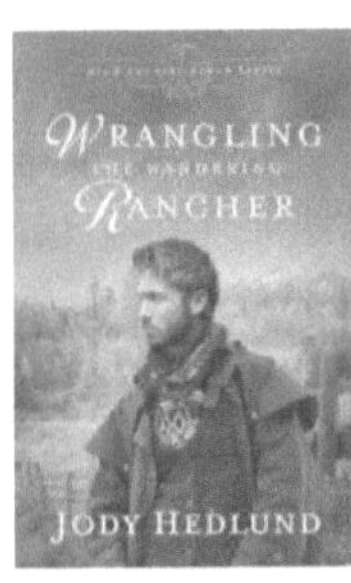

Wrangling the Wandering Rancher

Maisy Merritt has vowed she'll never marry a mountain man. Even though she loves the Colorado Rockies and the wild creatures she helps, she hates the way her pa's mountain-man ways take him away from his family. Maisy's ready to start a normal life, and that includes marrying a normal man. As a trapper and trail guide, Tanner Oakley lives a wandering life. He's decided that he's not husband material for any woman since he's so restless and unsettled.

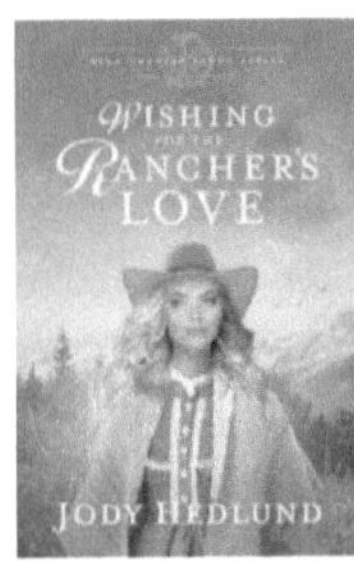

Wishing for the Rancher's Love

As the only one of her siblings who hasn't married, Clementine Oakley feels left behind. But she does her best to focus on her candy-making business in Worth's General Store. Giving and outgoing, she makes friends with everyone—except one person, the store owner's son . . . Grady Worth. Grady isn't sure why he can't get along with Clementine, but every time they're together, all they do is bicker. When his dad proposes a contest to encourage Grady to find love, Clementine is the last person he considers as an option.

Jody Hedlund is the bestselling author of more than fifty novels and is the winner of numerous awards. Jody lives in Michigan with her husband, busy family, and five spoiled cats. She writes sweet historical romances with plenty of sizzle.

A complete list of my novels can be found at jodyhedlund.com.

Would you like to know when my next book is available? You can sign up for my newsletter, become my friend on Goodreads, like me on Facebook, or follow me on Instagram.

Newsletter: jodyhedlund.com

Facebook: AuthorJodyHedlund

Instagram: @JodyHedlund

www.ingramcontent.com/pod-product-compliance
Lightning Source LLC
Chambersburg PA
CBHW022112310726
48972CB00007B/1997